The
Hollywood
Sisters

backstage pass

The Hollywood Sisters

backstage pass

Mary Wilcox

DELACORTE PRESS

The author thanks the brilliant girl readers at
the Windward School and Dorsey High School.

Published by Delacorte Press
an imprint of Random House Children's Books
a division of Random House, Inc.
New York

www.randomhouse.com/teens

Educators and librarians, for a variety of teaching tools, visit us at
www.randomhouse.com/teachers

Library of Congress Cataloging-in-Publication Data
Wilcox, Mary.
Backstage pass / Mary Wilcox. —1st ed.
p. cm. — (The Hollywood sisters)
Summary: Having moved from Anaheim to Hollywood, California, so her sister
can star in a television sitcom, shy and lonely Jessica tries to discover who is
selling unflattering stories about her sibling to the tabloids.
ISBN-13: 978-0-385-73354-0 (trade pbk.) — ISBN-13: 978-0-385-90369-1 (GLB edition)
ISBN-10: 0-385-73354-2 (trade pbk.) — ISBN-10: 0-385-90369-3 (GLB edition)
[1. Sisters—Fiction. 2. Self-confidence—Fiction. 3. Actors and actresses—Fiction.
4. Television—Production and direction—Fiction. 5. Hollywood (Los Angeles, Calif.)—Fiction.
6. Mystery and detective stories.] I. Title II. Series: Wilcox, Mary. Hollywood sisters.
PZ7.W64568Tel 2006
[Fic]—dc22   2005036536

Printed in the United States of America

10 9 8 7 6 5 4 3 2 1

First Edition

for Paul

This poem is for Ashton
Forgiveness I'm askin'
For the actions and errors
I made.

The bowl it did slip
When I loosened my grip
And went flying off,
I'm afraid.

Though covered in junk
You weren't being Punk'd
When I sloshed you
With peach marmalade.

HERE ARE FOUR IMPORTANT THINGS TO KNOW ABOUT ME, JESSICA ORTIZ:

⭐ I never get up before six-thirty in the morning, especially not during summer vacation.

⭐ I never ride in my sister's limo with her suck-up publicist.

⭐ I never go to my sister's set (not since the marmalade incident).

⭐ And, most relevantly, I got up this July morning at six a.m. to ride in my sister's limo with shoe-kissing Keiko so that I could make my first appearance on set since Ashton Kutcher had to towel fruit preserves out of his ears.

MY SISTER IS IN TROUBLE. I'M HERE TO HELP. SHE'S THE STAR, AND I'M THE SISTER.

Act I

In this business, fame lasts for a second. You can be blown up and be blown down. People keep losing interest in faces because new ones come along every single second. I'm one at the moment. Tomorrow I won't be. . . . It's about survival. If you're sad about it, then you're in the wrong job.

—KEIRA KNIGHTLEY

A white five-bedroom Spanish colonial house with red-tiled roof, pool, and patio, perched on the slope of Beverly Hills—the decorators have this place looking like the Ortiz family has lived here for years.

Don't let them fool you.

We first walked in the door two weeks ago; we instantly started thinking of our two-bedroom ranch back in Anaheim as the "little" house. Tapestries, crystal-and-wrought-iron chandeliers, soft leather couches—the place was photo shoot–ready from day one. I had to look twice at the polished silver frames to believe it was our family in the pictures.

As for the other things that money can buy . . . I knew about surround-sound stereos, plasma-screen TVs, and bedrooms that you didn't have to share with your sister, but there's money whispering in *everything* now—in the plush terry towels, shiny wood floors, smelly soaps not available at supermarkets, fresh-cut flowers—even the clothes in the closet belong to a cooler thirteen-year-old than me.

Anaheim to Beverly Hills is only forty miles on the map, but it feels like we've traveled a lot farther.

E's agent arranged everything—including convincing Mom and Dad that Eva needed to move closer to work. Mom is on leave from her job at the library, but Dad still makes the commute to the Ortiz Brothers' Garage every day. So far his only comment on the neighborhood is that you'll see more Bentleys here in an hour than you will in a year in Anaheim.

It's at this crazy-early hour that I first spot a real, live neighbor. (An alien would assume cars were the dominant life-form.) While having orange juice on the patio, I see a girl who looks about my age. She's wearing a white tennis skirt and top; her blond hair is pulled back in a smooth ponytail. Her tennis court lies off a path next to our pool. The houses are huge in Beverly Hills, but packed close together.

I'm not usually outgoing, but for a moment I have a mental montage of life with my new friend: We soak in my Jacuzzi, trade books in the hammock, and play with her dog. Or would she have a pony instead?

Taking a deep breath, I cut across the patio. "Hi, I'm Jessica. Your new neighbor. This is our house now."

"It's not yours."

"Well, we just moved. . . ."

"I mean, it's not *yours*. You *rent*."

I guess I didn't have to worry about the decorators fooling anyone after all.

Tennis Neighbor walks away swinging her racket.

I miss my best friend back in Anaheim.

I miss the things that money can't buy.

Sometimes I'm grateful to Eva, sometimes I'm not.

ou know Eva stars on ABC's highest-rated comedy, *Two Sisters*. You know she's up for Young Latina of the Year, and Sophie Cassala wants her for her next film. You might wonder if she's tired of being told she looks like a petite Jessica Alba. (She's not.) E lives at home with her family, and doesn't smoke, drink, or date anyone in a boy band. She's never checked herself into a hospital for exhaustion. She's nowhere near that kind of drama. Our parents even met at a church picnic!

But could you guess the one word that best describes her?

Fabulous? Lucky? Talented?

You're not even close.

Let me tell you, I'm the sister and I know. The word for Eva is: *driven*. Eva is totally, utterly, down-to-her-chromosomes driven.

Really? Eva? you say. *She seems so natural and easygoing.*

Well, that's because she is *driven* to appear natural and easy-going.

Do you know how many girls tried out for Eva's career-making role as Hottie Neighbor Number Two on *Two Sisters*? Five hundred eighty-four! There were girls who were prettier, and girls who were more talented, and even girls who were both, but none of those girls wanted to be Hottie Neighbor Number Two more than Eva.

And what about the fact that Eva turned HN#2 from a guest role into a recurring role into a starring role? You don't get there by walking; you get there by d-r-i-v-i-n-g.

"**Y**ou're driving me insane, Mom." Eva smiles when she says it.

"Listen, *m'ija,* there is only one way to handle a bully. And that is to face right up to her."

Mom and Eva enter the patio through the double doors that lead off the breakfast room.

Mom is holding a folded copy of Exhibit A in our investigation: the *Los Angeles Record*. We're facing the Hollywood version of a serious crime: image attack.

Genie Wolff's Hollywood Hype column shows a photo of Ashton postmarmalade, with a horrified Eva at his side. A female hand (mine) reaches from out of the frame toward the bowl. The text reads:

It's a Jam Shame!
TV teen Eva Ortiz left Ashton Kutcher in a jam during his recent guest appearance on *Two Sisters*. Hype has this question for Ashton: Orange you glad you met Eva?

It wasn't Eva's fault at all! It was mine. Also, he was hit with marmalade, not jam, and the flavor was peach, not orange. Could Genie care any *less* about the truth?

You might say: *Gossip columnists are people, too.*

I agree.

11

They're awful, greedy people willing to pay top dollar to get someone to squeeze sleaze on celebrities.

And this isn't the first incriminating picture to run in the newspapers. For the past month, Eva's been a tabloid darling, even though she's done absolutely nothing wrong. What's worse, whoever is feeding trash to Hollywood Hype has access to the *Two Sisters* set. There's no other explanation for the press leaks. I have some suspicions, and I'll be sticking to Eva's side till the case is cracked.

"Mom, don't worry," Eva says reassuringly. "Keiko said these kinds of stories get forgotten before they're even written."

Except by me—the girl who spent four hours drafting her apology poem to A.K.

FADE IN.

EXTERIOR SHOT: LOS ANGELES. SMOGGY SUMMER MORNING.
WINDING ROAD. WHITE STRETCH HUMMER ROUNDS CORNER,
PICKING UP SPEED.

*W*e're driving down the twisting roads of Beverly Hills. Even the streets are skinny here, so the Hummer is hugging the corners. It's Eva, Keiko, Mom, and me, with a driver on the other side of the tinted glass.

Eva looks relaxed and happy. You know her round hazel eyes, long brown hair, wide mouth, all set in a heart-shaped face. I share the same features—arranged less perfectly or more interestingly, depending on whether the glass is half full that day. Plus Eva has that something *extra*. Her hair isn't just long—it's impossibly long. (Seriously, a human head can't grow that much hair in only sixteen years; she gets extensions woven in every six weeks.) She's unreasonably fit thanks to her personal trainer. And her skin has a touchable glow thanks to her none-of-the-good-stuff diet.

Eva is prettier in person than on-screen, but don't ever tell her that. (Tip: When you meet an actress, say that she looks *exactly* as pretty as she is on-screen. If you say that she looks prettier in person, then she thinks her lighting is bad; if you say she looks worse in person . . . well, that's rude.)

Keiko rips up Mom's copy of the *Record*. "Forget the article, Eva! The gossips can't touch you! You're gorgeous, talented, beloved!"

If there's ever an exclamation point shortage, Keiko may have to stop speaking entirely. I mean, entirely!

"But, E," I say quietly, "the photo must have been taken by someone on set." When I was little I couldn't pronounce Eva, and I've been calling my sister E ever since.

"There are always different people roaming the set," Keiko says with a shrug. She peers through my not-a-star invisibility shield. "You look a lot like Eva today, babe!" She hands this comment over as if it's an expensive gift that a kid might not know enough to appreciate.

"Thank you."

"I really mean it," insists Keiko brightly, bobbing her choppy-cut, dyed-white hair. Her face makes me think of a piece of classic Japanese art framed in too-shiny silver plate. "Really!"

I nod. I stopped believing her two reallys ago.

You know that girl in school who scuttles from person to person gossiping and spreading stories? Well, Hollywood is a town where people are paid to do that. That girl? She's called a publicist. Publicists pressure reporters and columnists to get more of the right coverage (Superstar loves babies and sunshine!) and stamp out the wrong coverage (Superstar loves tantrums and drugs!).

"Keiko, the article wasn't true—" My mom still isn't happy.

"The *picture* was true. That's all people respond to. Believe me, it's nothing! Let this one go."

A publicist would let it go.

But not a sister.

The car stops and the driver opens the door. Keiko says, "After you, E!" She has worked for my sister for two months now, but this is the first time she's made a play for her nickname.

Eva is stepping out of the car, but looks back over her shoulder to say, with her "famous" smile, "Only Jess calls me that." And because Eva is Eva, there is no offense given or taken. Her voice lets Keiko know that she is now part of a family secret, and Keiko beams.

And me? I step out into the sunlight—it feels warm all the way through. A lot of Eva belongs to the world, but some things are just for me.

*A*large red light is attached to the wall next to the studio entrance. The light will flash to signal that filming is in process, so don't crash through the door and ruin a take! There's no flashing today because shoot night is Friday, with Monday through Thursday for read-throughs, script revisions, rehearsals, and costume/staging/camera preparation.

This entrance leads us directly backstage. On set, Mom heads off to review the week's script, and Keiko to bring a delivery to Craft Services.

Two girls run squealing toward my sister. You might know them as Eva's costars, Lavender Wells and Paige Carey. I'm thinking of them as Suspects One and Two.

After all, *they* were supposed to be the stars of *Two Sisters,* not some upstart from Anaheim.

I try to discover who the culprit might be by observing which one offers E the fakest compliment:

"Pilates is *so* working for you, sugar."

"Gwyneth didn't look as good in those shoes."

They both score perfect tens for insincerity. This isn't going to be easy.

"Hi, hi," says E. Air kisses all around.

Lavender eyes my striped cotton top, jeans, and Chuck Taylors. She is dressed in her signature color: purple Juicy tee, slim violet pants, indigo bangle bracelet, and sparkly amethyst hair clips. I guess it could be worse. Her parents could have named her Mauve. "You must be Eva's baby sister," she drawls. Her family left Georgia when she was eight, and her accent has been getting thicker ever since.

I nod. After all, I was Eva's sister the last few times we met, and nothing has changed.

Dark-haired, violet-eyed Lavender shot to fame as the winner of ABC's first Teen Sensation contest. She's so magnolia-sweet you could get a sugar rush from talking to her. "You look a lot like Eva." Lavender stares into my eyes. "Really, shug, you do."

Being the focus of Lavender's attention is not easy, but I know it will last for only another three . . . two . . . one seconds. And she is gone. Lavender is a confusing combination of enormous focus and tiny attention span.

Now Paige squints at me. She is a trend slave. Since this month's *Vogue* lists parsley as the new It Color, Paige looks as though she's been attacked by an angry salad.

She points to the book peeking out from my bag. I usually carry a book to hide behind. "That's so Jake," she says.

"Excuse me?"

"*To Kill a Mockingbird*? Jake Gyllenhaal's favorite book?"

It's on my summer reading list. "Everyone at school is reading it."

"Huh." Paige looks impressed. "I didn't know Jake was so popular."

Paige is usually cast as "teen girl, so pretty it almost hurts." With her huge green eyes, long blond hair, and perfect cheekbones, it's hardly a stretch. A former model, she loves fashion, but sometimes gets caught in the crossfire between stylists. That's how her Golden Globes ballerina-meets-biker-babe look happened.

Even among L.A. actresses, where gorgeous is average, Paige stands out. Here's a real-life example:

The lighting technician just got accepted at film school for the fall. The crew is gathering up breakfast, teasing him about losing all their phone numbers when he gets famous.

"I'll always have your number," the tech jokes to his boss, Lighting Guy Bob.

Paige joins in. "You'll be a rich director. Then I'll be sorry I called you a slacker who couldn't light a Christmas tree!"

The tech looks puzzled, but he's goggling with gratitude that Paige is talking to him. "You never called me that."

"Sure I did. I just never knew your name."

"It's Kenny."

"Kenny? That doesn't sound right."

Kenny gazes up at Paige adoringly. (Paige towers a good four inches over him.) Then he asks her to autograph his napkin, which she signs "Dear Kevin" because he looks like a Kevin to her.

"Thank you *so* much, Paige! You're the best!"

That's how pretty Paige is.

The Belle or the Beauty: which one wants the show to go on . . . without Eva?

wo Sisters, Thursday nights, eight-thirty p.m., ABC.
Here's how the new season is shaping up. Like last year, two sisters (Paige and Lavender) share a Boston apartment with their never-seen on-screen parents. The girls are high school

students by day, but battle a pet-napping ring by night. Last year, the parents went on a world cruise when the scriptwriters couldn't think of a way for them to not notice a family of emus in the living room.

Two Sisters was supposed to be all about two sisters. You've been more surprised, I'm sure. Then this neighbor chick (or should I say, *chica*?) shows up, and starts to steal the show. There's a reason that the showbiz term is "steals the show" instead of "improves the show" or "saves the show from certain cancellation." That reason is jealousy—Hollywood is awash in it. The tide of jealousy is never out.

Some shows have thrived when an unknown grabs the spotlight. The "two sisters" know they've got a good thing with Eva's booming popularity, but the jealousy is still there. I think one of the sisters has convinced herself that the show can go on without E.

But which one?

scene 4

"I'm glad you came to the set today." Eva is eyeing the food table, choosing among flavored water, sparkling water,

20

and water water, bypassing the Krispy Kremes completely. "No one even remembers the Ashton incident."

Behind me, I can hear the producer, Roman, whistling "Lady Marmalade." At the other end of the buffet, Lighting Guy Bob nudges the punch bowl away from me.

Maybe you've seen the photos of Eva buying out the store at the local Krispy Kreme? The captions are always something like: HOW CAN EVA CHOW DOWN THE HOT-'N'-GLAZED AND STILL FIT INTO HER SIZE-SKINNY JEANS?

Let's just say that *TeenStyle* isn't exactly employing a crack investigative team. Eva buys pounds of Krispy Kremes because Lighting Guy Bob loves them—and Lighting Guy Bob has more to do with how Eva looks on TV than the entire hair and makeup staff combined. As for Lighting Guy Bob—with his belly and white beard, he's more size Santa than size skinny.

Does Craft Services like Eva dishing out the eats? Not a bit—it's their job to manage food and beverages. But they only provide E with life-sustaining nutrition; Bob delivers a soft halo of beautifying light.

This Monday morning, the cast gets ready for the first read-through of the week's script. The actors sit around the *Two Sisters* living room: couch in front, stairs behind, entrance to the kitchen stage right, and front door stage left. You've seen the layout on every network comedy—it gets people in and out of the action and allows for lots of different camera angles.

Right now the four main cast members are holding scripts and highlighting their speaking parts. Lavender, Paige, Eva, and the only guy in the cast, Jeremy Jones.

Jeremy plays the boy next door, on this sitcom and two previous ones just like it. Blue-eyed with shaggy blond hair, he hangs out with the crew instead of the actresses. He's in the new ad for Gap, and it's not one of their happy-dancing ones, but a moody, black-and-white montage of him walking Sunset Strip. Past the Viper Room, the House of Blues, Tower Records, then right down the middle of the street, with the Hollywood sign glowing in the background. (Not upbeat, but I bet it's selling shirts.)

Keiko is always trying to snap photos of Jeremy and Eva looking cozy.

The inside scoop is: they work together.

That's it.

But magazines want to show something buzzworthy; they're bored with pics of Eva at another hug-a-kid charity event. The possibility of Eva and Jeremy closerthanthis gives E a little juice. Keiko sends out the photos, and then denies dating rumors so vehemently that even *I* start to think she's covering up.

Jeremy is not off the slander suspect list, but I can't see him . . . bothering. He doesn't compete with Eva for roles, and he's been on TV since he was a baby. This show is just what he's doing from now till next time.

Lavender and Paige still look like the prime suspects to me. Each frowns, watching Eva highlight the most lines this week. Again.

The producer plus some writers, studio executives, production crew, and the director join the actors. The cast will read through the script as though they're performing each part. There is even someone narrating the stage directions and making incidental noises like approaching footsteps or cat meows.

It's a good time for me to drift into the background, investigate, and enjoy a cinnamon twist.

Behind the scenes on the set, the crew is laying new lines of cable. Assistants run past, chatting into headsets. A pair of studio types are taking a tour.

"Oops, sorry!" I burst in on two camera techs playing Grand Theft Auto on a TV in the props room. I keep moving, discovering random leftovers from the fake life of the show: a working minifridge filled with plastic food, a huge wardrobe with only a couple of plush emus shoved in the back.

All is quiet in Hair and Makeup and the dressing room corridor, so I head back toward the stage. I watch the crew take the living room wall and spin it around to reveal a brick-faced "outside" wall with shutters. The rooms are as reversible as sweaters, creating the illusion of lots of different spaces. Everyone is laughing and getting along. That could be an illusion too.

The set is a busy place: There's Craft Services, the crew, the actors and their teams, the producer, the director, maybe some on-set tutors or studio people. Since the show stars underage actors there are usually family members around—my mom and I are with E, Lavender's mom is with her (yes, she's the one in the Team Lavender purple sweatshirt), Jeremy's mom and little brother show up sometimes. Paige is an emancipated teen (i.e., she divorced her parents), so she has different agents spending time with her.

How can I find the person selling slander about E? Or is it *people*?

What do I know about the culprit? Only the three things she has to have, and I'm not talking about fashion accessories:

⭐ **Motive: Jealous of E? Or needs money that gossip columns will pay for stories?**

Opportunity: Access to the set
⭐ **Means: Camera to take incriminating pics**

Okay, that's narrowed it down to . . . everyone that I've seen around me all day. Scooby Doo made this whole sleuthing thing look a lot easier than it is.

I scribble notes in my clue-collecting pad.

"Find something interesting?"

Uh-oh.

Jeremy Jones slides up beside me. He must not be in the scene that's being read now. He pushes his blond hair off his forehead.

"Um . . ."

Words desert me.

If speech is a superpower, surprise conversations are my kryptonite.

"Top secret, huh?"

I nod. At least the nod is still with me.

I want to say something so that I sound like a smarter, funnier, better-dressed version of me. Is that too much to ask?

Jeremy pulls at his hair again; the length is annoying him.

"Haircut?" I get out.

"I need one. But my agent says I can't. This is 'my look.' "

"Won't it still be your look if you get your hair cut and it's still you?"

Jeremy gives a half smile. "I asked him the same thing."

"And?"

"He grunted. Agents and philosophical questions—bad mix."

Pause.

With nothing to fill it.

Finally Jeremy says, "You're Eva's sister, right?"

I nod once more.

"A Hollywood sister, huh? What's your thing? Acting, singing?"

"I don't—bad voice—I go to school."

"Modeling school?"

Best.

Question.

Ever.

This is the single nicest thing anyone has *ever* asked me. Until he adds, "Hand model? Foot? Kneecap? Everyone's modeling something."

I shake my head. "I'm just visiting Eva."

He lifts an eyebrow. "But what if you accidentally get 'discovered'?"

"That's exactly what I *don't* want." The confession slips out. Before Jeremy can ask me more questions, I spot a familiar face over his shoulder: square jaw, friendly grin, salt-and-pepper Caesar cut. "Is that George Clooney?"

"Yeah, he's this week's very special guest star."

"I guess the director wouldn't—"

"Let you within five feet of him? True. But George is getting together a pickup basketball game later. You could meet him then."

"He's heading this way now," I say.

At that moment, Lighting Guy Bob notices me. And practically body-slams George to a halt.

"Let me get that donut for you, Mr. Clooney," he insists.

The crew is a *tiny* bit superstitious about my bad luck on the set. Of course, *I* don't believe in jinxes, the evil eye, or self-fulfilling prophecies. Avoiding sidewalk cracks, throwing salt over your shoulder, not saying the words *Lord Voldemort*—all hokum.

Nonsense.

Hot air.

So could you please be the one to knock on wood for me?

The whole Jeremy conversation—not exactly fluid. Let me explain. I am not shy. But . . .

Sometimes I freeze up talking to people. And my face gets warm—I can see the air around me getting wavy from the heat.

Sometimes I can't pay attention to what's being said because I'm trying to think up something to say if the conversation turns to me.

Sometimes I make excuses to avoid public-speaking situations. (*Sometimes* in this case means "whenever possible, barring acts of God or my Abuela.")

Sometimes . . . I am shy.

Shhh . . . I'm not supposed to say so, though.

Shy-denial came about because my mom read a book—an occupational hazard for librarians. She has for sure read too many books with titles like *Why So Shy?* and *10 Ways to Blame Yourself for Your Daughter's Shyness*. One of the "action steps" that stuck was that I can't label myself as shy. It sends a message "not only to others, Jessica, to yourself as well, that shy is all that you are.

That people shouldn't expect you to talk, or contribute, or even *be* anything special." I think my mom had a cheat sheet for that pep talk.

So, here's how I'm supposed to put it: I'm polite. I'm caring. I'm sensitive.

If polite, caring, and sensitive mean that talking in front of people makes me want to shrink so small I can hide in my own pants pocket, then, yes, that's me . . . Little Miss Sensitive.

I'm happier in the audience than onstage. And, last I looked, there were a lot more of us in the audience than there were jumping around under the spotlights. And who would all those stage types be showing off for, if there weren't people who were curious, who wanted to observe, who wanted to find out what happened next?

E asked me what the worst thing about being shy was, since it's a foreign language to her. I knew the answer instantly even though I hadn't thought of that exact question before: *You can't hide it.* The laser beam of attention heats up over your head, and you have to be "on."

A nice thing about E?

She's always "on." She draws all the nibbling eyes so I can be free.

"**W**hy are *you* after me? Why are *you* after me? Why are you after *me*?" Eva is practicing her line readings while she gets fitted with an elegant purple gown.

Hélène, the petite French costume supervisor, is on her knees adjusting the hem. Her blue eyes flash in her delicately boned face. "You young women—growing taller! It should not be allowed!"

"Carolina outdid herself this time," Eva says happily.

Her Carolina Herrera halter gown flows straight to the ground, cinched at the waist and clipped on one shoulder with a beaded strap.

Hélène snorts. "For fifteen thousand dollars she should have. Hélène will be double-locking the costume room tonight."

Whoa. That's more than my mom's car cost.

Maybe it's worry about my new school full of Tennis Neighbors, but I'm open to some fashion advice. "Any fashion tips, Hélène?"

It's hard to understand her with the pins in her mouth. I think she says: "Burberry is overpriced plaid."

Not helpful.

I get hit with a sudden flash of missing my best friend.

Leo Takashi—where are you?

There are some great things about a guy best friend—he never cares what you're wearing; if you feed him, he forgets what he was mad at you about; he's glad that you want to write the female speeches in his zine (*Anaheim Avenger*); and he is always up for a bike ride (even if he just washed his hair).

There is one bad thing.

When you move away, he doesn't keep in touch.

I keep my eye on Lavender and Paige all morning.

Lavender is not giving me much to watch. She's flipping through *Vogue* and stretched out on the set's easy chair like a skinny spill of grape juice.

Paige is wound up and restless. She's been making phone calls nonstop and now has Roman Capo cornered with complaints. Roman is not just a producer; he's also the show runner. Just as a school principal is responsible for getting kids educated, Roman is responsible for getting the show made every week. The main part of the job seems to be taking all the problems on the show and keeping them in his ulcer.

I slide closer to Paige so that I can hear their conversation.

"Eva is in the Carolina Herrera gown for that scene, so why do I have to wear overalls?"

"That's where the funny is, Paige." Roman doesn't even lift his eyes from his BlackBerry. "Eva is attending a formal dress party, and you and Lavender pretend to be gardeners to crash."

"But couldn't Carolina design the overalls? She would make *amazing* overalls. People would want to be married in those overalls."

Roman cuts her off. "Regular overalls are funny. And funny is money, babe." He checks his watch. Dropping his voice, he says, "Keep an eye on the time. You have a lot of dirt to dig up, and Genie said her photographer would be there at eleven sharp."

Digging up dirt?

Genie?

Photographer?

Did Project Stop Slander just bust wide open?

Paige and Roman head out the side door.

I follow as quickly as I can.

I'm pushing open the heavy metal door right behind them when I'm . . .

Caught.

Nabbed.

Trapped.

In the blue-eyed stare of Jeremy Jones.

"Going somewhere?" He is definitely suspicious of me, but why?

We step outside. The sunlight is harsh after the dim studio. The door shuts behind us. We watch Paige pull away in a golf cart driven by Roman.

Jeremy and I survey the scene. No one else is around.

It's only us and a couple of extra golf carts.

And for a moment all my shyness is so much steam whistling out of a kettle.

So just because a golf cart is parked at the door, and just because you can see the keys are in the ignition, and just because you're pretty sure you can figure out how to operate it, is that any reason to pursue your sister's slander-slinging costar in a stolen (or at least heavily borrowed) vehicle?

Well, I think so too.

"I'm going for a ride," I tell Jeremy.

"What?" He could not look more surprised.

I get in and turn the key. The golf cart shakes to life under my hands.

"That's not a good idea," Jeremy says, but he jumps into the seat beside me just as the cart lurches away from the curb. The gas pedal seems much more sensitive than the brake on this thing.

Paige and Roman have disappeared down an alley. I step on the gas, and pretty soon we're topping five miles an hour. From the corner of my eye, I can feel Jeremy staring at me. "Are you trying to break into stunt driving?"

Why is he convinced that I hang around my sister for the sole purpose of launching my own career?

I never know what he's going to say next.

Unfortunately, what he says next is, "Look out!"

Followed by: "Was that George Clooney?"

OH.

FREAKING.

NO.

Sadly, it was Mr. Clooney, out playing a friendly game of pickup basketball with the crew.

By the time Jeremy and I get the cart turned off and jump out, Mr. Clooney is insisting that he is fine, that the cart only grazed him, and he's sure an ice pack is all he needs. Fury is rising off the crew like steam off a volcano, but Mr. Clooney is very understanding.

Then *everyone* on set pours onto the lot. I didn't even know that many people worked on *Two Sisters*. Lavender, Eva, Keiko, and—yipes—Mom push through the crowd.

Mom puts her arms around me, stroking my hair. "Are you all right, Jess? What happened?"

I can't answer her.

As I watch Mr. Clooney bravely limp away, all I can do is silently take back everything bad I said about *Batman and Robin*.

scene 7

Two Sisters wrapped a bit early today: Mr. Clooney wasn't available for script run-through.

Back at home, Mom and I are sitting on white lounge chairs beside the pool. (It still feels good to say "the pool." At our old house, we could sit beside "the driveway" or "the tree swing"—not the same.) But even the pool can't cheer me up tonight.

"How is the apology coming?" Mom asks.

Not very well:

> I'm sorry with all my heart
> For hitting you with that cart.
> You could've complained,
> but chose not to.
> Get better soon;
> you've got to.
> Don't think the show a bad gig.
> Hugs to your potbellied pig.

Yikes. Let's hope he's still on painkillers when he reads this.

Eva comes outside and flops down on the chair next to mine. For a while, we sit watching the sunlight change the colors of the pool.

I breathe in chlorine and lilacs, and I can't take it anymore— living this life my sister has pushed us into, and knowing that I keep messing it up. "Go ahead. Say it, E. Say what you're thinking."

I'd rather have her blast me than sit here beating myself up.

"Huh? Well, okay." Eva twirls a long tendril of hair around her finger. "I was thinking that acting is like jumping into a pool. It's totally absorbing. The constant *buzz-bang-buzz-what?* of your brain shuts off. Everything you were thinking about has to go at the moment of impact. Like swimming, acting is physical—why do people forget that? They think it's like some kind of mind trick, when *inhabiting* the character's body and mind—they're two parts of the same whole."

Okay. She didn't blast me.

Then again, did she even notice that I mowed down a major movie star today?

"Eva," Mom says, "you know what your sister is asking."

E reaches over and squeezes my hand. "Lighting Guy Bob says George is fine. Just a big, manly, cart-stopping bruise."

I turn to E so that she can see my face. My apology tumbles out in a rush. "I'm so sorry about today! E, I can't believe—"

"Jess, it's all right. Accidents happen."

"Yes—all the time! To me! Why is that?"

"Maybe . . ." Eva picks her words as carefully as her next role. ". . . you get lost in your own thoughts . . . and you're not paying full—"

"I was *detecting,* Eva. By definition that means paying full attention."

"Detecting?"

Busted. I hadn't wanted anyone to know what I was doing till I could show some results. I'm the one who made the mess and I want to be the one who cleans it up.

"I'm looking into some things. That marmalade photo in Hype was taken on the set. Someone there sold you out. And I don't think it was a random stranger."

Mom and E exchange a look.

Mom says, "That's why you left the house? For Eva?"

I nod.

Eva jumps in. "Jess, what a great idea. You're a natural detective— you're always paying attention to people, noticing things that I never would. I need you to keep looking into this."

"Am I even *allowed* on the set?"

She smiles. "Everyone knows the Fabulous Ortiz Sisters are a team." Yes, that was the name of our two-sister band. When we were seven and four, we had a band with one plastic Mickey Mouse guitar. The other sister (read: me) got to shake a box of rice. "Say yes, Jess."

Eva hits me with the full power of her smile.

Which isn't playing fair.

"Yes."

"I feel safer already."

Mission accomplished, Eva picks the revised *Two Sisters* script out of her bag and starts to read.

The writers have tailored the scenes to how the actors read them this morning. Of course, Mr. Jealousy comes up here, too. The actors jealously scan the scripts to see whose role has been cut down, who got the better laugh lines, etc. Tomorrow, they'll rehearse the revised scenes, the writers will tweak, and couriers will rush out re-revised scenes. Rinse and repeat until shoot night.

In moments, Eva is lost in *Two Sisters* TV-land.

"Hello! Hello!" Eva's trainer appears, walking around the house. Barun is short, bald, energetic, and heavily muscled. He looks after Eva's fitness and nutrition. Right now, she's on the Green Diet. She can eat anything green in portions of her palm or smaller.

"Let's go, Miss Eva! You're going to tone those arms, and I'm going to burn your ears with the hottest story in town."

Barun isn't a gossip. He's trying to break into soap opera

writing. (Did you know people *aim* for that?) He has a hugely successful gym right off Rodeo Drive, but everybody has to be a hyphenate in Hollywood. Trainer-writer. Waiter-actor. Pool boy–director. Maybe the town should be called Holly-wood.

Mom and I head inside. Once, we got inspired to join Eva for her Pilates workout. *Once.* Never again. I had jelly legs for a week.

"Jessica, about today . . ."

"Please don't tell Dad, okay?"

"Your father wants to be informed."

"Then why isn't he here?"

Running his own business keeps Dad away a lot. "Honest mechanics have to work harder than the other guys" is his excuse. It used to be whenever I got in trouble, I could say something about Dad not being around and Mom would rush in to make me feel better.

Those were good days.

Unfortunately, Mom is not quite as behind the times as her L.L. Bean comfort-fit jeans would have you believe. "Jessica, I know that the move, the change in our *vida*, hasn't been easy." She gives me a long look. "If you wanted to show me any of your poems, I'd be happy . . . very happy to see them."

"Mom, I'm not writing . . . those poems anymore. I'm helping Eva now. I'm actually *useful*."

"Useful?" says Mom. She looks bewildered. "*M'ija*, you're wonderful."

I don't respond. I go back to work on my apology.

But there really isn't anything nice that rhymes with *George,* is there?

When I was younger, and was trying to tell Mom something, I'd slide a note into her bag when she left for the library. I copied the idea from the notes she put in my lunch. Hers used to rhyme, too. I can still remember one:

> *I before e except after c
> Is a spelling rule
> That's always helped me!*

(I guess I remember that one because the words *weigh, height,* and *ancient* were on that week's spelling test. Weird, huh?)

Mom sometimes guesses right about me. I have been working on a new poem.

But I won't show it to her.

If you have to drive,
Keep the guest star alive.
I'll be back on the set—
They haven't banned me there yet.
I just need a clue
To play my part.
Protecting the people
Close to my heart.

Mom, I'd show you this rhyme
But what could you do?
You're worried enough;
You just moved too.

I wake up disoriented. Again.

I look around the room. *My* room.

It must be my room because the cream-colored throw pillows on the low turquoise chaise spell J-E-S-S-I-C-A in pale yellow letters.

But the place isn't familiar yet.

It's not that the decorator didn't bother to take notes when she interviewed me about my "dream room." Though she didn't.

It's not that the furniture is new—though it is. The look is a funky twist on traditional Spanish villa decor—natural wood furniture, accented in a vivid shade of turquoise. My bedding, dresser, and tilting mirror are all turquoise, with dark wood accents and swirling carvings.

None of that is what throws me off.

It's the aloneness.

Thirteen days of having my own room versus thirteen years of sharing with Eva. Takes some getting used to.

I walk downstairs to the kitchen.

"Good morning, Jessica."

Our housekeeper speaks with a musical African accent. It feels wrong to think of her as coming with the house—like the Jacuzzi tub or the flat-screen—but she was here when we arrived. Today her headdress is a vibrant gold, matched with dangling globe-shaped earrings and a patterned dress.

She has the coffee brewing, the pancakes on the griddle (for me, Mom, and Dad), and Eva's breakfast in the blender (an unidentifiable green sludge, prescribed by Barun).

"Morning, Mali. That's a pretty dress."

The brilliant red, gold, and green pattern wraps around her from floor to shoulder.

Mali nods once in acknowledgment.

I haven't exactly figured out how to talk to Mali. She's always cordial, but never too friendly. Is she so definite about sending the "business relationship" message because we're all so awkward about it? (Not counting Eva—who would be comfortable considering the entire human race as her extended staff.)

"Mali is a pretty name. What does it mean?"

"It is not the name I was born with. I chose it when I came to America to remind me of my country."

"What country are you from?"

"Mali."

"Oh." Translation: *Doh!* How do you apologize for never having heard of someone's entire nation?

Mali does not seem offended. She is either naturally placid, or has low expectations of Hollywood teens. She waves a spoon toward the table.

"Morning newspaper is there."

I open the paper.

And despite the delicious smell of batter and blueberries on the griddle, I lose my appetite.

There in the Hollywood Hype section of the *Los Angeles Record,* a terrible headline faces me:

Fore Shame!

Reckless golf cart driving "putt" movie star George Clooney out of action on the *Two Sisters* lot.

Breakout teen Eva Ortiz offered apologies for the

unforegivable treatment.
Let's hope she makes her
next smash hit on the TV
screen!

There is a photo of Eva looking upset while Mr. Clooney grips his leg.

The Hype continues.

Digging Up Dirt

Model-actress Paige Carey
was also making an impact,
breaking ground at a new
playground for underprivi-
leged children. At "The Mud
Pie Zone," the gorgeous
girl got "carey-ed" away,
gleefully mixing dirt at
the tot lot. Maybe her costar could take a "paige"
from her book?

Paige's picture shows her muddy—and not one bit less gorgeous for it—and hugging adorable toddlers.

I drag my eyes back up to the Eva-Clooney photo.

The only good thing about the photo is that it eliminates a suspect.

Paige can't be the slander leak because she wasn't there to take the picture.

Act
II

You can be true to the character all you want, but you've got to go home with yourself.

—JULIA ROBERTS

A morning that started out terrible gets worse.

A lot worse.

Mom and Eva are gathered around the breakfast room table reviewing the Clooney article over coffee and green sludge.

I'm not sure how Mali could be three feet away, calmly chopping celery, and not feel the tension of a young actress smeared in the press, her guilt-stricken little sister, and their worried mom, but she gives zero sign of interest. Life in Mali-land either takes place a million miles from this kitchen, or she's a better performer than my sister.

The phone rings.

Don't answer it, I want to say. At six-thirty in the morning, it's already been that kind of a day.

"Hi, Keiko," Mom says. "Thanks for going to the set so early. . . . Are you sure? . . . Could it have been misplaced? Taken out for cleaning? . . . Is Hélène all right? . . . Okay, we're on our way."

Mom hangs up and explains: Eva's Carolina Herrera gown was stolen. All fifteen thousand dollars of it.

Rather than wait for the limo, Mom decides to drive us to the lot. We're rolling down the driveway when Tennis Neighbor appears, looking us over.

Most days I don't think about the fact that Mom is still driving her old Nissan Maxima. Today I do. (When Eva gave Mom a *Two Sisters* bumper sticker last season, Mom said she was saving it for a better car.) Dad plans to keep the Maxima alive *forever*. It's a point of pride with mechanics to keep their cars running for hundreds of thousands of miles, past their prime, and past the point where you want Tennis Neighbors to see you sinking down on the gray fabric seats.

Mom has other things on her mind. "I wasn't able to clean the bedroom this morning."

Eva groans. "Mom, that's Mali's job."

"I know it is. But I don't want her seeing everything a mess."

"She doesn't *see*. She cleans. You've done more cleaning since she started than you ever did at the little house—which makes no sense."

Mom grips the steering wheel. "Since when do you tell me what to do in my own house?"

We ride the rest of the way in silence.

With just some floating, unspoken words taking up the oxygen in the car: *Since it's not your house anymore.*

At least Dad is consistent. Our old car gets us smoothly through the traffic and onto the set. It will live to embarrass me another day.

Keiko, Lavender, Paige, Roman, and Hélène are already gathered in Wardrobe when we three Ortizes arrive. The room features thick binders of fabric swatches, a dressmaker's dummy, dozens of outfits on rolling bars, and a very upset French costumer.

Hélène is almost in tears. "We rented the dress for the week. I kept it double-locked all night. When I came in this morning, it was here. Everything looked fine."

Roman awkwardly pats her back. "Don't be upset, babe. The insurance will cover it."

Keiko asks, "What happened next, Hélène?"

"I brought Jeremy's new shirt down to him, we talked for a few moments, and I came right back. The dress was gone." Hélène presses the heels of her hands against her eyes. "Roman, is Security on the way?"

Roman looks uncomfortable. "I didn't notify Security. We'll hand this right to the insurance company. Mr. Banks is going to be on set soon, and I don't want the place overrun with rent-a-cops. Banks is going to see a smooth operation."

Ivan Banks owns *Two Sisters'* production company and he's the primary moneyman for the show—i.e., he's Roman's boss, i.e., he's *everybody's* boss. Banks was recently married and is bringing his new bride for a tour of the set. She's a huge fan of the show. (If you think that means the bride must be *much younger* than the groom—you're right.)

"Were the overalls stolen?" Paige asks hopefully.

Hélène shakes her head.

"Now, that's a crime," Lavender says. She is wearing an indigo halter dress. Her earrings, kitten heels, rings, and handbag are all in various shades of (wait for it . . .) lavender.

"Do not pretend you are unhappy about this, Lavender," Hélène says, her emotions getting the best of her. "You were so angry that Eva was going to be wearing 'your' color."

Lavender looks startled for a split second, but her face smooths. She doesn't look at Eva; she speaks to the air: "*As if* she could wear it like Ah do."

She glides off, purple heels clicking.

There's more bustle as Roman tries to calm Hélène, and everyone else throws out possibilities for what could have happened to the dress. Lavender's perfume is starting to fade from the air (I know you can guess the scent) when everything gets a whole lot . . . creepier.

Beep-beep.

I step outside the dressing room. I pull my phone out of my bag and flip it open.

And then I really wish I hadn't.

```
View message from:_____
View
Ignore
```

*W*hen the text message pops up on the screen, my first thought is that Leo has finally gotten back to me—even though the sender's name is blank.

I hit View. And even when I read the message, I first think that Leo is making some kind of joke that I don't understand.

But Leo and I always get each other's jokes. We just do. And we'd never think a message like this was funny:

```
I know what you're doing.
Stop now.
```

There is no callback number.

There is no way for me to know who sent the message. Or why.

Does someone want to end Project Stop Slander before it even starts?

Is the message really meant for me?

If someone is threatening me, does that mean I'm threatening her?

My first thought is to tell Mom, but when I look into the dressing room, I see she has her hands full dealing with Eva and the stolen dress.

Besides, Mom already gave her advice: There is one way to handle a bully. Face right up to her.

The message gives me a queasy feeling, but I push that aside. If Lavender is looking for someone easy to scare, she picked the wrong sister.

I charge out of Wardrobe and back to the stage area.

A small knot of men in jean shorts, baseball caps, work shirts, and construction boots—Rocky the director, Larry the director of photography (boss of the cameramen), and Lighting Guy Bob— are all looking over a layout of the kitchen set.

I am not afraid to talk to them.

I am *not* afraid to talk to them.

Grr . . .

Why did Eva have to get all the acting ability in the family? I can't even convince myself.

The casual interrogation. It's a skill.

That I don't have.

"Where was I when the dress was taken? That's what you're asking?" Lighting Guy Bob stares over his belly at me. Santa never looked so angry. "What's it to you?"

Rocky and Larry start laughing. "I'm sure Bob was lurking over the Craft Services table, like always," Larry says. "Do those donut crumbs count as evidence?"

Hilarious. Not.

Next, I visit Hair and Makeup. The stylists were together having breakfast when the dress was taken, but nobody else (i.e., Lavender) was with them.

I don't bother checking in with Paige, since the playground photo cleared her, or with Jeremy, since Hélène said she was with him.

Lavender is the person I most want to talk to, but when she sees me coming toward her dressing room, she closes the door. Loudly.

"Did you want something?" Across the hall, Jeremy stands just inside his room. He watches me stare at Lavender's shut door.

"No, I—well, I have a couple of questions." I turn to face him, stealing a peek into his narrow room: iPod Bose system, Play-Station, TV, laptop, piles of graphic novels. . . .

Jeremy faces me head-on, spreading his elbows. His short-sleeved, surfer-casual shirt is baggy enough to block my view. "A *gossip column* career? That's what you want? You came to the wrong place for that."

The concept of a sister helping her sister seems foreign to this guy.

I ignore his gossip crack. "When you and Hélène were talking, did you notice anything? Anyone walk by?"

"I didn't notice anyone." Jeremy narrows his eyes at me. "And you can quote me on that."

"Okay, I'll move along." Glad to!

The room next to Jeremy's is used for staging. I knock and enter. Kenny, the technician, has a large white light projecting onto the wall. He is working with different colored filters, producing rainbows of light.

"Hi," he says. "Can I help you?"

"I'm Eva's sister. I—I was wondering if you saw anyone strange hanging around earlier. When the dress was stolen?"

Kenny shakes his head. "I've been in here, working with this light all morning. Door closed. Sorry."

From behind me: "Is she bothering you, Ken?"

"No, Jer. It's fine."

Jeremy walks around me to put his body between Kenny and me. He rests his hand on top of the light and looks directly at Kenny. " 'Cause if she's bothering you, let me know."

"She's a nice kid, Jeremy. No bother." Kenny has to lean around Jeremy to give me a wink.

The good news is that the *Two Sisters* set has a protector.

The bad news is he's protecting the set from me!

scene 3

CSI Beverly Hills—would that team just quit a case if everyone was rude to them?

No, but they might stop by their sister's room for a pep talk.

Eva isn't in her dressing room. So I wander all over backstage looking for her. I pass the emu wardrobe and see that it's been locked. A gold push-button combination lock is looped through the door.

Sure, now they start worrying about theft. The gown is already gone and so is a chunk of E's reputation!

I find Eva in one of the small conference areas that double as tutoring rooms. Eva takes classes through an online homeschooling program called Laurel Springs, and also shares tutors on set. She is seated with a *Your Mexican Heritage* book, back issues of *Latina* magazine, and her laptop.

Paige is next to her, scrolling through the playlist on her iPod.

I try to slip in quietly, but Eva's teacher turns to glare at me. He has thick gray hair; dark, almond-shaped eyes; and a scowl. "What are you here for? Driving lessons?"

Eeps. I guess he was in the crowd at the Clooney carting.

Angry Tutor isn't saving his sourness for me. He rolls his piercing eyes to my sister. "Eva, the assignment is to study local Mexican history, but you keep turning it into an acting exercise."

Eva shrugs. "I can learn all the history stuff, but I'll write it up in the voice of my character."

Paige jumps in. "Oh, can I do that too?"

E stifles a groan. "Paige, listen to me. You are not taking this class." Eva turns back to Raúl. "So, what do you think? Can we do it my way?"

Raúl frowns, working something over in his mind. Under his breath—but he wants us to hear—he says, "Just trying to decide how desperate I am for money." He sighs. Deeply. "Pretty desperate. You win, Eva. Again."

Even back in Anaheim, Eva could get people to accommodate her. The last year before *Two Sisters,* she was getting lots of work—commercials, small roles—and she was always able to get teachers to e-mail her assignments, or friends to bring her books to the house. People tend to do things for her.

I guess even more now that they are on her payroll.

There's a knock, and Jeremy comes in. He can barely see over the top of an enormous bouquet. "Paige, there you are. These are for you."

The flowers aren't your average dozen roses. They don't have a scent but are a gorgeous blend of rich pinks and reds, with pointed petals. Paige doesn't pay much attention to the flowers. Probably because there's a Kitson shopping bag looped around Jeremy's wrist.

"For me?" Paige jumps up. "Kitson is my favorite!"

Once Halle Berry was photographed leaving the store with an *H* initial handbag, all the copycat celebrities had to shop there too.

Jeremy puts the bag on the table . . . and notices who else is in the room. "Don't open it here, Paige," he says, his eyes on me.

She flashes him a look. "Why? What's in the bag?"

"Don't ask me." He's still looking at me. "They were left outside your door. By a secret admirer."

He takes Paige and the flowers (she's gripping the Kitson bag) and practically pulls them both from the room.

Raúl sighs. "All right, Eva, where were we before the fascinating soap opera of celebrity love interrupted?"

"Knock-knock!" Keiko and Mom appear at the door.

"Hello, Raúl," Mom says. His frown deepens.

"Eva, they're blocking the scenes now. Then we've got a lot of work to do!" Keiko says.

"Work?" says Raúl.

"There's an interview at the Ivy lined up, and we've got to get Eva pretty pronto. Prettier!"

"Work," Raúl repeats bitterly. He gathers his papers and briefcase and stomps to the door. "Secret admirers and now *pretty* work."

"*Adiós,* Raúl," Eva calls after him.

Once the door bangs behind him, I have to ask, "E, what's his problem?"

Keiko answers, "Don't worry about Raúl, babe!" She drops her voice and talks close to my ear. "Maybe he's sad that *he* doesn't have a secret admirer."

And then—weirdness.

Keiko gives me a nudge with her elbow and a huge wink.

As if we have a secret.

When what I'm starting to think is that Keiko and I are the only ones around here *not* sharing a secret.

Mom taps her watch. "Eva, let's get the blocking going. I want time to go over the questions that might come up in the interview."

I have a question: Raúl Hernandez, where were you when Eva's gown was stolen?

scene 4

Mom, Keiko, and I sit in the theater part of the set to watch the blocking. The actors rehearse, and the director begins to figure out camera placement. The camera assistant places tape on the floor wherever the cameras stop.

Rocky holds a viewfinder in front of his eye, trying to isolate what the camera will see. When the show finally shoots, the technical part will involve a dozen different lighting instruments, large cameras mounted on wheels, microphones attached to booms (long metal arms), and more.

Blocking can be interesting to watch if the director has the scene laid out visually in his mind . . . or it can be like today.

"Hold up, everybody." Eva, Lavender, Jeremy, and Paige freeze like dolls. "I don't like where that camera is."

A low groan sounds from the actors and the assembled camera and lighting crew. Rocky never takes ten minutes when twenty will do. Roman stands in the wings, tapping his watch furiously.

Eva gestures for me to sit with her on the set couch.

"Go ahead, Jessica," Mom tells me. "Keiko and I are just going to be reviewing publicity photos."

I walk to the stage, and—ignoring Jeremy's suspicious glance—sit beside E. The actors unfreeze to gather around the living room table.

"I hate sitting around," Eva says. "It's the worst."

"You think *this* is the worst?" Lavender says. "When Ah did mah first TV movie, *Goodbye Dragons,* Ah had to recite hours of sobbing speeches to a laser dot aimed at a rock." (Computers would later add the dragons.) "Don't leave me! Don't leave me, laser dot! You'll break mah heart!"

Eva laughs, then says, "Okay, I can top that one."

Everyone leans in.

"A couple of years ago, I volunteered to act in this U.S.C. student film, *Angst, Angst, and Bile.* You know, to get more camera experience? I played all different parts—a drug addict, a runaway, an amnesiac. I went to this place of horror and despair for days."

"It made you depressed?" Paige asks.

"No, I loved it! The horrible part was that they got a C-minus on the project!"

Everyone laughs, even Eva. (But really she's still mad about that grade. Which was a D.)

Jeremy says, "I can top that." We all moan. You know a guy is going to have a gross story, don't you? "I had a cameo on *General Hospital,* playing a sick kid. To act like I was vomiting, they made me a mixture of breakfast cereal that I would have to hold in my mouth and spit up."

"Ewww!"

"And the worst part . . ." He pauses for effect. "We had to do twenty-five takes of the scene!"

"Noooo!" The moment is more dramatic because the lighting crew is testing out different filters, and Jeremy's face shines in an eerie blue.

"True story," says Jeremy, smiling. "*And* I was only three years old."

Oh.

The three-year-old part makes it all feel sad.

Fortunately . . . there's Paige.

"I can top that!" she says. "I was in this commercial for sandals, and I had to wear pink golf knickers and walk up and down Rodeo Drive on a warm, sunny day."

"What's so terrible about that?" Eva asks.

"Didn't you hear me? I said *knickers*! No one looks good in those."

I laugh—even though Paige probably looked amazing as always.

"And this other time," Paige continues, "I had to keep dead chicks in my pocket because I was acting with real hawks and needed to hold their attention." My mouth drops open, picturing the scene. "But, c'mon, knickers? That's horrible."

"What about you?" Jeremy glances at me.

Silence.

Sudden.

Awkward.

Now Jeremy looks embarrassed. I can tell he just remembered that my story is about being a jinx.

Keiko saves the moment, stomping onto the stage with her hands clapping, chop-chop. "Interview time, Eva! Stand-ins will have to finish the blocking. Time to hit Hair and Makeup!" There isn't an official photo shoot with this interview, but Keiko believes in being camera-ready at all times. Lavender's mom comes to get her next, and Jeremy and Paige follow.

I see Mom still in the theater seats, finishing up her own conversation . . . with Raúl Hernandez.

Mom walks over. "Let's go, Jessica."

I try to keep my voice light. "What did Raúl want?"

"He was apologizing for being brusque earlier. He's under strain, you know. Usually, he's quite polite."

Or was Raúl looking for an excuse to hang around, gathering gossip?

"*G*ive them a smile and they'll leave you alone," Keiko advises.

A paparazzi photo can be the price of admission at the Ivy. Set up like a country cottage, the Ivy is one of the most celebrity-centric restaurants in the world. Its dining rooms are filled with antiques, fresh flowers, and famous faces.

After a few poses for the photographers perpetually hanging out across the street, we meet the *TeenStyle* reporter and get seated on the patio, ringed in by the ivy-covered picket fence.

While the reporter gets her recorder ready, Keiko and my mom whisper last-minute advice to Eva. Keiko's tips are all about positioning for bigger, broader roles ("Mention that you dance! Mention that you sing!"); Mom's are all about protecting E ("Don't mention where you live").

The actors are gathered around one table with the reporter. I'm seated at the next table over with Mom, Keiko, Paige's agent, and Lavender's mom. Mama Lavender has dark hair and violet eyes, set in a full face; her lilac T-shirt spells out LAVENDER'S MOM in curlicue letters.

The reporter turns to the actors. "Can you describe what it's like working together on season two of *Two Sisters*?"

Paige jumps in. "We're like a baseball team. No one player can catch the ball by herself."

The reporter blinks. Moves on. "What is daily life on the set like?"

"Oh, shug, every day we appreciate each other and respect each other. We're not here to judge, we're here to enjoy each other's company and workmanship." Mama L. smiles with pride.

"Eva, is it true that Sophie Cassala is pursuing you for her new film?"

Lavender blurts out, "Lots of people are reading for *Wisconsin Girl*!"

Lavender's mom pastes on a smile and whispers to mine, "It's so great that your Eva is going after the part."

Mom shakes her head and whispers back, "Her father and I gave that a firm no. The script is too mature—profanity, *nudity*. We'd never let Eva appear in *Wisconsin Girl*."

The reporter hasn't overheard the moms and is still after E. "*Are* you in the running, Eva?"

69

My sister gives a mysterious smile. She'll never admit that she's not up for the part. "*Two Sisters* is what I'm concentrating on now, and I love it. Playing to a live audience every week, making them laugh." She sighs, lowers her lashes. "But a sitcom is always about the joke. Movies can bring your work to another level."

"Plus you can have different roles in movies," adds Paige. "Like brunettes. Or redheads."

Paige's agent clenches his jaw. "Just smile," he mouths at her.

"A dual role would be amazing," says Lavender. "Evil twin and all that."

"So *Sixth Sense*," Paige agrees. "Like when Bruce Willis played the psychiatrist and the ghost."

I think the surprise ending of that movie would still be a surprise to Paige.

"Everyone's playing dual roles," Jeremy says in a low voice. "All the time."

The reporter latches on. "Would you care to expand on that, Jeremy?"

"No."

"Oh." Pause. The reporter checks her notepad. "Who has gotten the most fan mail?"

No one wants to admit the truth.

I don't think even Genie would run this story: the most fan mail ever for a one-week period went to . . . Schmoo, the orphan emu from last season's cliffhanger. Nothing against the *Two Sisters* team—that little guy was insanely cute.

"We're not competitive like that," Lavender says smoothly. "Ah know Ah'd send fan mail to all mah costars."

"Paige gets the most love letters," puts in Eva.

"From anyone we know?" asks the reporter. Her eyes are on Jeremy. He doesn't answer; he lets the moment get long and uncomfortable.

"Don't ask about my new bag!" Paige says abruptly.

The reporter looks at Paige. "What about it?"

"It's from Kitson. That's all I'm saying." Paige is clutching a Be&D denim sling bag; it's been dyed a deep parsley. Someone was on the right page with that gift.

The reporter looks frustrated. "So, it's a big lovefest on the set. But without any actual—love?" Now her eyes are swinging between Jeremy and Eva. Keiko purrs happily beside me. Another rumor taking root.

The reporter doesn't ask the big question I have on my mind: If everyone is best buds at *Two Sisters*, then who sold out my sister . . . and her dress?

Mom's cell phone starts to vibrate, rocking across the table. "Hi, honey . . . what fax? I didn't send you a fax . . . ?"

I get Mom's eye and nod toward the street. I know she assumes that I'm going to the Kiehl's shop across the street (free samples!), but I'm actually going to take a quick walk down the block. Lucky for me that the A-listers like to shop where they eat. Kitson is just down the road.

Kitson is so popular that there is a red velvet rope with a security guard set up on the sidewalk to manage the crowd. The line is moving quickly today. I slip into the boutique to get a look at everything that is just about to be popular: vintage tees, cashmere halters, rhinestone flip-flops.

I spot Paige's new sling. Price tag: $1,150.

"May I help you?" the saleswoman asks.

"I heard that Jeremy Jones was here this week—buying this bag?"

"Jeremy? No way. I'd have heard about that." I don't ask myself why I'm suddenly relieved. "But the other stars of the show are in all the time—Paige and Lavender. Are you a fan?"

"Um . . . I follow them." I browse for a bit, watching the shoppers chat on their bejeweled Sidekicks while looking over the "You Were Never My Boyfriend" T-shirts, mink cell phone cases, and pink pompom boots. I'm about to invest my own nine bucks in a bottle of

Karma Guard (*What Goes Around Comes Around*) when I check my watch and realize I've got to hurry back to the Ivy.

I tell myself that I was investigating the bag as part of Project Stop Slander—not out of nosiness. After all, I'm not out to sell gossip—despite what Jeremy thinks.

The word *gossip* echoes in my mind—but why? Nothing E (or I) did today could ricochet back on her.

Right?

scene 6

I'm eating some of E's twelve-bucks-a-box veggie cereal out on the patio when I almost choke on the green mush.

Paper open in front of me, I'm facing strong proof that Project Stop Slander is not going precisely as I had hoped. First, Hollywood Hype features a photo of Eva—at least, it looks an awful lot like an awful-looking Eva. Second, this item accompanies the photo:

Packing Her Bags?
Rumors fly that TV-teen Eva
Ortiz has been caught in a

Hollywood whirl of fast living. Check out our exclusive
photo—the bags under her
eyes would qualify as carry-
on luggage! Eva, your friends
at Hollywood Hype hear your
cry for help. We care.

Ugh. Even for Genie Wolff the gak factor is pretty high. I'm re-gretting having breakfast before reading the column when E bounces outside. She's still in her short cotton pj's. (No one else in the family will appear pj-clad in front of Mali.)

"Where did Genie get this picture of you?" I ask, waving the paper at her.

Eva takes a quick look. "Oh, that's not me."

"Hello? Are you seeing this big-eyed, brown-haired girl here? She's got the Ortiz chin and Abuela Lucia's hazel eyes, so who do you think she is?"

"That's Lilly."

All actors are part crazy. The whole thing where they "pretend to be someone else." That's not a normal occupation. But Eva used to be able to keep her crazy in check. Now, though . . .

"Don't you remember Lilly? The heroin addict?"

"You mean from *Angry, Angry Smile*?"

"*Angst, Angst, and Bile*. Obviously, my portrayal was not as unforgettable as I thought."

Eva takes a quick read through the column. Then she says: "Gak."

We head into the kitchen, and E gets on the phone with Keiko. Keiko promises to get Genie to print a retraction. But the retraction will go in a small box under the obituaries—the appropriate place for burying something.

Mom enters the kitchen. She takes a glance at the Hype; then she starts tossing around the orange juice and clattering the plates.

Mali takes no notice, just sets a new place at the breakfast table.

Eva clicks off with her publicist. "Keiko is on this now. She's starting to take the whole Hype thing more seriously."

Mom doesn't say anything. Her shoulders are stiff, and her face is set in tense lines.

"She's going to call over to the U.S.C. film school library—see if they have a record of who's been checking out the student films. That should be a good lead." Mom slaps the bread into the toaster. "Mom, Keiko will take care of this."

"Eva, that's not what's bothering me right now."

"It's not?" Eva looks surprised. "What is it?"

"Wait till your father gets here."

I shrink back behind the fridge. Am I in trouble, too?

There is only ever a two-word response to "wait till your father gets here":

"Uh" and "Oh."

scene 7

*M*y dad loves to fix things.

And he loves things that are fixable: cars, appliances, gadgets. Pop 'em open, pull out the broken parts, throw a wrench around, put 'em back together. If they light up and roll around, you know your work is done.

Not exactly the same process for raising two teenage daughters.

I'm not saying that Dad hides out under the hoods of all those broken-down cars—or that he hides out behind Mom here at home—I'm only saying that he likes to stick to work that he's good at. He likes to feel sure.

Maybe it's the same way that I don't like to go into a room and just start talking to people. Unless I have a sure purpose.

E used to get mad at Dad sometimes ("You missed my Skippy Peanut Butter audition! My best acting ever!"). He would try to make it up to her, but he didn't even know what "it" was. He'd usually buy her a chocolate bar—which was kind of sad, because she can never eat chocolate without breaking out, and kind of sweet, because you know he thought of it on his own—and tried to reach out without getting edited by Mom.

Dad comes down the stairs. He has a piece of paper in his hand.

Instead of all of us sitting down for breakfast, Mom tells me that she and Dad need to speak privately to Eva.

Which is my cue to go upstairs and listen beside my vent. They're talking about my Project Stop Slander investigation, and I can't even be in the room!

Mom begins. "Eva, do you know why I'm so upset?"

"I . . . figured it out."

"Your behavior is a huge disappointment to me."

Eva's behavior? I can't believe Mom would believe any of Genie Wolff's lies! I'm about to race downstairs when Mom continues.

"Eva, when you began working, we had a simple agreement. Your father and I would let you pursue a career, provided that we retained final say over what projects you accepted."

What is up?

Could it be that perfection-in-Prada Eva Ortiz has made a big mistake?

"Were those rules unclear to you?" Mom is sounding like a character in one of those legal dramas she loves to watch. That's not a good sign. "Was I unclear when I said Ms. Cassala's project, while artistically meritorious, was too mature for you?"

Meritorious? I don't think Mom has ever been "meritorious" mad at me. This is serious.

"You were clear."

"Is that why you faxed your father at the shop to get his approval after I said no?"

She *what*? The deal is, a parent has to sign off on all projects till Eva is eighteen, two long years from now.

"My agent thinks—"

"Your agent? Your *agent* thinks?" Mom's voice vibrates through the floor. "What does *your agent* think about your entire *familia* uprooting to help you with your work? What does your agent think about your father fighting hours of traffic to get to his garage every day? About me leaving the library before my pension vested?"

"Mom—"

"Your mother is speaking, Eva."

There is a moment of silence below. Then . . .

"What does your agent think about your sister struggling—leaving her home, her best friend?"

More silence.

"I'm sorry, Mom." Eva does sound sorry. Her voice is as tremulous as it was in the "Adieu, Emu" episode.

"I hope you are, Eva. You're running out of people who will say no to you, and that's a dangerous thing for a sixteen-year-old girl."

"Your mother's right," Dad says.

"I'm sorry. It won't happen again."

"I'll be expecting you to come up with an appropriate consequence for this, Eva." (Mom has some strange ideas about discipline. We pretty much have to come up with our own.) "I think that's all I have to say. Robert, do you want to add anything?"

He doesn't say anything.

Then I hear Eva climbing the stairs—a half second closer to eighteen with every step.

Down below, Mom and Dad are still talking.

"Rob, I don't know. . . . One daughter sees only what's right in front of her; the other sees everything *but* what's right in front of her."

I'd like to hear the rest, but there's a rap at my door. I dash off the floor and onto my bed seconds before Eva enters.

If I was expecting my sister to look tearstained or shaken, she doesn't deliver. I can see that she's unhappy to have her plans upset, but the narrowing of her eyes, the set of her chin, tell me that more than anything, she has moved on to the next thing on her agenda.

I want to ask her if she's still going to go after that Cassala movie.

But I don't.

Eva gives a small smile. "Who has annoying parents?" She flops down next to me on the bed.

"You do," I say.

"You too," she says. It's our old joke. Not so funny this morning.

"I tried to get Dad's permission to go after the Cassala role."

I paste on a surprised look. "After Mom said no?"

She nods. "I want that part. That's not a crime, you know." She pauses to see if I'm going to argue with her. I'm not. "So I have to think up some kind of consequence and I thought you might help?"

My first thought is that she wants *me* to take the discipline, but then I realize she just wants some ideas to get this episode over fast.

"Well, Mom sounded so angry—uh, I mean, from what you've told me. You're going to have to do something big to get her to forget this."

"Forget?" Eva has a thought. "You know Paige is cochair of this Adopt-a-Stray event this afternoon. I could help her with that. Tell Mom that my behavior was what? Selfish? So I'm working with this group to . . . remind me to think about others?" She bounces off my bed. "I've got to get Keiko on this now."

Is it only in L.A. where a talent for spin-doctoring helps in dealing with discipline?

"Thanks, Jess. We'll hit the set in thirty, okay?" She's gone as quickly as she came.

I lie on my bed thinking. About how the most interesting conversations happen after I'm told to leave the room. About how even in our brand-new lives, my parents keep trying to be our same old parents. About if Leo will ever call me back. About how much Jeremy can't stand me. About threats, text messages, a stolen dress, and Hollywood Hype.

But it's one thought that leads me out of my bed, through the French doors to my terrace. I look out over the glimmering pool, our landscaped gardens, and farther off to where the buildings of L.A. are shining in the sun. And I think: how far will Eva go to get her dream?

The question makes me restless under my skin. I had thought she already had it.

scene 8

*E*va's dressing room is thin and cramped, but the day the producers put a silver star on the door for her, she cried real tears. (Though that may have been for the benefit of the *Entertainment Tonight* camera crew—my sister doesn't just start working when they say "action.")

One wall is mirrored, and there is a closet for E's personal clothes, a thin couch, and a small window looking out onto a parking lot. A low desk holds her TV and laptop. A yoga mat is pulled out in the corner; since relaxing is about the only thing that makes Eva anxious, she uses the mat to do ab crunches.

As Eva, Mom, Keiko, and I push into the room, it fills up fast, especially with noise. Those three are still in their morning talk-plan-BlackBerry-cell-phone frenzy, so I sit back on the couch and notice . . . a square gift box on E's desk. Printed in black across the top is the word *Danger*!

Okay, the word isn't actually *danger,* as in D-A-N-G-E-R.

It's *danger* spelled C-H-O-C-O-L-A-T-E.

My sister loves chocolate, but practically has an allergic reaction to it. The makeup crew had to do a two-hour spackling job after her last Godiva breakdown.

And speaking of breakdowns . . . Eva is throwing a fit. "Why do I have to ask *Paige*? Don't the Adopt-a-Stray people want as much publicity as they can get?"

"Yes," Keiko says, "but we want Paige to be happy you're there! So the publicity will be positive."

She doesn't say *for a change.* But we all hear it.

Eva throws a look at my mom. But there is no help there. Mom thinks a thick slice of humble pie is exactly what E needs in her diet. "Explain it to Paige like you did to me, Eva. How you're so excited to see needy dogs get a good home."

Eva must have pulled out an Oscar-worthy performance to sell that to Mom; Dad and I are the animal lovers in the family.

While those three are talking, my cell phone *beep-beep*s.

The sound used to mean Leo to me.

Now it means dread.

I flip open the phone.

```
View picture from:_____
View
Ignore
```

The big blank space where the sender's number should be gives me a chill.

Part of me wants to hit Ignore.

But if I was an Ignore kind of girl, I wouldn't be in this mess in the first place.

I hit View.

A picture starts to fill the screen.

I don't know what kind of horrible image to expect. Something violent? Threatening? Purple?

I see the back of a girl walking down a corridor. She has brown hair and is wearing Keds, jeans, and a blue T-shirt.

I look down. At my blue shirt, jeans, and Keds.

The girl is me. And the picture was taken behind my back about ten minutes ago, as I was walking to E's dressing room.

Three words run under the picture:

I'm watching you.

I try to tell myself that Lavender has starred in one too many Lifetime "girl-in-peril" movies. But that doesn't stop the shiver tickling over my bones. I think Lavender is the slander-slinging leaker (and the *freaker,* the only name for someone sending messages like this). But what if I'm wrong?

I could handle the mouth from the South, but what if I've stirred up someone more serious—like Raúl Hernandez?

I click my phone off and can barely concentrate on what's happening around me.

I see Eva give Mom the Big Brown Eyes.

But it's no go.

E's the one in the doghouse; she's going to have to talk to Paige herself.

Mom checks her watch. "Keiko and I have a phone call scheduled with people at U.S.C. film school now. Please have this settled before we get back."

"It's too late to update the Adopt-a-Stray tip sheet, but there should be good coverage set up already." Keiko bobs her white hair. "Great coverage!"

The tip sheet is a list of celebrity guests planning to attend an event. Publicists send it out to the media before the event. The general rule is that A-list stars attract the biggest media vehicles (*Entertainment Tonight, Teen People*), but B-list stars work harder—pose for more pictures, stay longer, make fewer demands. Eva is about a B+.

Mom and Keiko head out looking serious. They are trying to find out if a librarian at U.S.C. helped anyone find the *Angst, Angst, and Bile* pics. The "Packing Her Bags?" slam has finally focused Keiko's attention on Project Stop Slander.

The door shuts and E sits down next to me on the couch. I'm worried that she'll notice how rattled I am by the text threat, but she has her own agenda.

She gives *me* the Big Brown Eyes. What's up?

"Jess, you're a dog lover. Maybe you could talk to Paige?"

"Me?"

I could not be more surprised.

Until suddenly I am.

More surprised.

"Hey, where'd that box go?" I get up to look around her table.

"Box?"

"There was a box here. When we came in. It said"—I lower my voice—"Chocolate."

"There was no box." Eva gets up from the couch and swings her bag over her shoulder. "If you don't want to help with Paige, you can come out and say so."

I *don't* want to help her with Paige, but that's not the point.

Eva is turned toward the door so I pull her shoulder till she turns back.

"I saw a box."

Our eyes lock.

"There was no box."

She almost convinces me with just a look.

And I have to wonder, did Mom or Keiko take the box? Or is my sister a great actress? Or am I just plain cracking up?

"**P**lease, Paige, I'm in trouble about . . . something. And my mom is not going to get off my case till I log some charity hours."

"Need to rehab the image, huh? That's tough," Paige says. "I totally saw it coming."

Eva sighs. "C'mon, Paige. Can I come to this Adopt-a-Stray thing with you?"

I know my sister. She's asking Paige for a favor in a place where she can get lots of eyes on them—the crew, Lavender—so that Paige will have a hard time turning her down.

Paige smiles almost sincerely. "Sure, Eva. You can crash my publicity. Again." She pauses. "I'm kidding! But you do."

Paige is going to make Eva work for her favor.

While everyone is watching their drama, I think it might be a good time to take another look around backstage.

I keep my eyes open. There is the usual bustle around the area right behind the stage, with things quieting down as I move farther toward the storage rooms. It smells like sawdust back here; the walls are unplastered, rough wooden beams crossing each other.

I find the emu wardrobe—its lock is gone. With no one around,

I take a quick look inside. Nothing has changed. It's mostly empty, with just the few emus stuffed in the back.

I look closer.

Something shiny catches my eye—did one of the emus' plastic eyes fall out?

No . . . it's not an eye.

It's a bead.

A silver bead like the one on the shoulder clip of the stolen dress.

A random visitor to the set didn't rush the dress out of here that morning. The dress was hidden in this wardrobe until it could be smuggled out later.

Someone had planned the whole thing. Someone on set. Someone who works with Eva every day. Someone obsessed with all things . . . lavender?

I close the wardrobe and look all around it, feeling along the top, kneeling in the dust to look under the bottom.

Nothing.

I stand again.

Then, right at my eye level, off to the side, I see a flash of metallic gold. Where two beams cross, something has been tucked away, almost hidden. . . .

The push-button lock that I had seen on the wardrobe.

I pluck out the lock and feel its weight in my palm. Too late I think that maybe the police could have dusted it for fingerprints. I had the same kind of Guardian lock for my locker last year. I can't resist punching in my old locker combination: 8–0–8.

Nothing.

I put the lock back carefully. If it was hidden, maybe the thief is planning to use it again?

I take one last look into the wardrobe, shaking the emus and watching another bead fall to the ground. I put that in my clutch too.

The open door of the wardrobe is blocking my view, so for a moment I can't place the angry voice that says, "What are you doing?"

I peek out.

"Or should I say, what are you doing *this time*?"

scene 9

eremy Jones is staring me down. It's way too late to throw myself into the wardrobe and pretend he isn't there.

I take a deep breath.

The casual lie. It's a skill.

That I don't have.

"I'm . . . uh . . ."

"Snooping?"

"No!" *Well, yes. But not the way you think.* "Jeremy, do you seriously think I would sell out my own sister for cash? Fame?"

The cool look in his eye says he does.

Which says way more about Jeremy than it does about me.

"Well, I wouldn't, okay? I'm trying to . . ." I don't want to get into Project Stop Slander with Jeremy. Hélène cleared him of stealing the dress, but I'm not sure how tangled this scheme is. Or how crazy Jeremy will think I am if I try to explain. "I'm trying to be a sister to my sister. Not launch an acting career, or a gossip column, or, or *whatever* you think."

He looks at me for a long moment, then says: "Singing."

"What?"

"Singing career. That's what you're hanging around for. You have the look."

I give him my best glare. He doesn't even blink. "So you believe everything I've told you is a lie? That I'm using my sister to get publicity for my own . . . what? Band?" (Band names fly through my head: Gotta Getta Glare, Doubter Boy, Suspicion.)

"You heard me."

And if he didn't look so entirely superior when he said it, I would not have to do what I'm going to do.

"All right, Jeremy. Remember you asked for this."

"For what?"

For this.

I inhale from the diaphragm . . . and belt out the *Two Sisters* theme song, in my best Gwen Stefani style:

Are you a sister?
Can't resist her!
Can you speak, see, go?
Are you a sister?
Can't resist her!
Be a sister,
Let it show!

Jeremy raises his hands in a sign of surrender. "Whoa."

I think I proved my point.

"That was *terrible*." In chorus class in Anaheim, there were the altos, the sopranos, and the Jessica-please-just-turn-the-music-for-Miss-Baxter.

"I told you."

"That was gears grinding over gravel. Man, who would think a cute girl had *that* inside her?"

Was that a compliment wrapped in an insult?

Or the other way around?

Jeremy smiles a real smile at me for the first time. All the way up to his eyes. I'm smiling too. Until he adds, "You'd better stick with foot modeling."

"I told you—!"

"Joking, Jessica." He looks at me curiously. "I believe you. About the singing. But you're definitely up to something. . . ."

And then a shy spasm hits.

All I can do is look at the stuffed emu still in my hands. Please be one of those people who assumes quiet people are smart. Please. Please.

The moment stretches. And stretches. Until I'm saved by the . . . *beep!*

Jeremy's watch beeps. He checks the dial. "I've got to go."

He doesn't, though. The watch beeps again.

"Okay, Jessica. I'll see you." He heads back across the set.

I toss the emu back into the wardrobe, closing the door with a click.

For a moment, I have a strange feeling—as if Jeremy Jones would rather have stayed with me.

*P*ettable pooches, here we come.

Mom, E, and I are riding in the back of a white Town Car toward the beach. Palm trees line the boulevard leading up to the Santa Monica Pier. The amusement park—Ferris wheel, roller coaster, arcade, carousel—comes into view.

I am having a sulk. To no avail. "Fine, keep your secret. I don't care."

I so *do* care.

I caught Mom and Eva whispering. But they won't tell me what's up. I guess why shouldn't they have a secret? Everyone else does.

Mom and E are all smiley-smirky with their hidden plan. They don't even seem too upset that the conversation with the film library was a bust. No one remembered helping to find Eva's awful *Angst* photos, but the librarians said there are often lots of students around, doing their research unassisted.

We step out of the car. Competing with the crash of waves is the sound of dogs barking. The Adopt-a-Stray event spills out from the pier to the beach. Photographers are everywhere, and I get a sense that the pier was chosen more as a backdrop than because it's the perfect place to have dozens of orphan dogs.

I should be worried about what E and Mom are cooking up, but the sight of all those dogs makes me too happy.

My sister and Keiko hurry over to where Paige has already attracted snapping photographers. Mom follows them, and I lean over one of the pens to play with the puppies.

A dog handler approaches. "Are you Eva Ortiz's sister?" she asks.

I nod.

"Wow. What's that like?"

That's what everyone asks.

I want to ask them: "What's *not* living with her like?" I've never tried it.

I respond with the Keiko-approved script. "Oh, Eva is fantastic. Just like her character on *Two Sisters*."

The dog handler nods. "That's what I thought. I could tell that was the real her on the screen."

It is the real her. It's just not the only real her.

And speaking of her . . . my sister approaches, Mom at her side, with an intense look in her eye. Has she figured out that I'm wearing her new Lacoste polo? I casually place my palm over the incriminating alligator.

"You need a dog," Eva tells me.

I sigh. "Like Mom would allow that."

Mom tenses her shoulders. "Mom would."

Whoa.

Anaheim Mom said she couldn't deal with a dog in the house, all the cleanup and care. But Beverly Hills Mom has people to help with that. Keep your limos, swag bags, and pampering professionals—a dog would be the best perk ever!

"We're getting a dog!" I shriek. "Really?"

Eva puts on her best Hollywood accent. "Hey, babe, who's your sister?" Then she sweeps her arm toward a round wooden pen. "Keiko picked out the best hound around."

Mom looks alarmed. "What kind of dog is that? Besides *big*."

A Great Dane pads over to us on four enormous paws. He has a smooth, dark brown coat, pointed ears, and watchful eyes. I pat the Great Dane and wander around to the other pens, observing carefully.

It's like I tell E, you don't pick a dog like it's a handbag on the shelf.

You wait.

Till you're sure.

Till you see a face, wrinkled, pudgy . . . perfect.

"Her," I say. I kneel down and a squat little English bulldog toddles over and licks my hand as if she knows me. As if she likes me already.

And that's how I wind up with Petunia.

"But what about Chocolate?" asks Eva.

"Chocolate?"

"That's his name—he's a chocolate Great Dane." Eva reaches into her bag and pulls out a square box.

I've seen it before.

In her dressing room.

Today.

"Keiko had this rush-designed this morning for the photographs." Eva opens the box and holds up a thick leather collar that says CHOCOLATE in silver letters. It would fit around Petunia's waist.

I pull Petunia closer into my arms. Eva shrugs. She gives the box and collar to Chocolate's handler.

Keiko rushes over with a photographer in tow. "A bulldog?" she whispers to Eva. "That's not on-trend at all. Big is the new little! A Saint Bernard or maybe a Scottish deerhound . . ."

I give my sister a look: On-trend or off-trend, Petunia is my dog. So Eva flashes her camera-ready smile, and the photographer snaps a few photos of her with the world's best bulldog. Keiko is trying to get him to take more pictures, but he is distracted by Paige's squealing.

"Another gift?"

Is there a perpetual rainbow over that girl's life or what?

Paige faces a delivery guy from the set. He hands her a small bag from Fred Segal and a bouquet of sunflowers and gladiolus.

"Read the note, Benny," Paige says.

"Um . . . it's Kenny. 'Sunflowers for Paige, no one could outshine you.' "

When am I going to be gorgeous enough to continually mangle a guy's name and still earn the puppy eyes from him?

Paige tears into the Fred Segal bag. Inside the bag is a jewelry box. And inside the jewelry box is a sparkly pair of earrings. The earrings dangle with diamonds and sculpted gold-and-topaz sunflowers.

The secret admirer strikes again. And just like with the Kitson bag, the gift itself is a not-so-secret clue.

Act III

You kind of stop growing at the age you are when you become famous. Because what happens is, people start removing all your obstacles, and if you have no obstacles you don't know who you are. You don't have real perspective on the problems that face you in life, how to surmount them, and what kind of character you have.

—GWYNETH PALTROW

enie Wolff has finally run a flattering piece on Eva, so why aren't I happier?

It's Puppy Love!

Every dog has its "tale." Eva Ortiz had planned to attend L.A.'s Adopt-a-Stray day just to help draw attention to the worthy cause—but an English bulldog had other plans. "You can't pick a dog like it's a handbag on the shelf," explained the TV teen and new puppy parent. "You have to be sure." This dog's life will be anything but ruff!

Petunia is stretched across my lap. I run my hands over her soft ears, and she looks up at me, panting happily.

We came home from Adopt-a-Stray to find the Kennel Cab from Pets of Bel Air driving away. Keiko had ordered everything in the store. My room is now accessorized with dog toys, vitamins, brushes, grooming tools, and a first aid kit.

I love it all, even the enormous plush doggie bed with CHOCOLATE silk-screened in brown letters.

Mom's contribution is a pile of books on everything from *Daily Dog Care* to *Amazing Facts About Animals*.

Eva calls me, and I scoop up Petunia against my body.

I don't know why Genie's article got me down. I know better than to believe what's in the gossip columns.

*I*n Eva's dressing room, Hélène is fitting E with her replacement gown. Hélène herself created the knee-length silk jersey dress. The color can only be described as utterly, completely . . . lavender.

When I see the glint in Hélène's eye, I know it's no accident. If she suspects that Lavender had something to do with the Carolina Herrera theft, she'll dress every actor, actress, and animal in purple from now on. Each accessory will be purple, down to wads of grape-flavored bubble gum.

I open E's laptop and Google Lavender Wells. My plan is to write down every relevant number that comes up (dates, addresses) and try them all on the push-button lock.

Lavender's fans seem to know everything about Lavender . . . and they still like her. They love her!

The sites have tons of Lavender pictures, quotes, excerpts from interviews, amazing graphics, and music. One has a complete analysis of her horoscope. Another has a reading of her palm—picked up from a telephoto picture of her waving. A third is a collection of letters to Lavender, who is referred to in each letter as "my best friend." A fourth features the "I Love Lavender" theme song. Set to the tune of "Take Me Out to the Ballgame."

Spoiler alert: I'm including the actual lyrics of the song below. They will spoil your appetite, so skip to the next paragraph if you're due to eat soon.

Lavender, you're my hero
Girls round here
think I'm zero

But if you show up
at the prom with me
I'll go down in
Park High hist'ry.
So it's hope, hope, hope
for the big day
If you don't come it's a shame
For it's one, two,
three times I'll ask
Please go out with me!
[refrain repeats]

(It's hard to believe a guy with such a strong tenor voice couldn't get a prom date.)

Where do these fans get their information? Pet peeves, family history, virtual tours of her hometown in Georgia, school photos, and constant mentions of her favorite book. (*Harold and the Purple Crayon*, of course.)

There are even photos of Lavender and Jeremy looking cozy, with lots of "are they or aren't they a couple" guesses. My guess is that Lavender's publicist thinks just like Keiko. But Lavender and Jeremy do look so . . . smiley together, especially in a group of luau photos.

Strange. The show never filmed in Hawaii.

I pull back and focus. All I'm looking for are numbers.

Birthday.

Street number.

Area code.

Zip code.

Behind me I hear:

"Ooch."

"Excusez-moi."

"Ouch."

"Pardon."

Eva clears her throat to get my attention. She nods at Hélène. Hélène has one eye on where she's pinning and one eye on the computer screen. There is a huge banner flashing "Lavender Wells #1 Fan site!!!!" And I haven't been able to turn off "I Love Lavender," either.

"Ouch."

"Pardon."

Agitated Frenchwoman does not like what she sees.

I power down, grab my bag, and head for the door. Hélène is instantly more attentive to her task.

"E, I'll—"

"Yeah, good idea," Eva interrupts. Her look tells me, *Go. Now.* "I'll catch you later."

With E recovering from her pinches and pokes, I move forward with my investigation.

For the stolen dress, I have Hélène clearing Jeremy. Unless he was stalling Hélène while a partner stole the dress? For the Clooney pics, I have Paige in the clear. Lavender still has motive and opportunity for the Ashton, Clooney, and *Angst* leaks as well as the stolen Herrera.

I only have one real lead so I head right to it.

Once again, the back part of the set is deserted. Walking down the twisting hallway, I spot the large wardrobe. Getting closer, I notice that it's not only unlocked; it's ajar.

I'm certain that I left it closed yesterday. Closed tight.

I start to hurry toward the wardrobe, and am almost in touching distance when . . .

Blackness.

The lights go out.

"Hello?" The windowless hallway is completely dark. Farther away, I can hear people calling for Lighting Guy Bob. Time to earn his nickname, I'd say.

Nearby I hear . . . footsteps?

I stumble, disoriented. I reach out both hands, groping along the rough walls toward the wardrobe. Suddenly my fingers brush against a warm . . . something.

No.

Not something.

Someone!

"Aaaagh!"

I jerk back my hand, but it's too late.

Strong fingers whip out and grab my arm.

"Let me go!" I'm wrestling and pulling against the grabber. "Let me go!"

I can't twist free.

"Shhh, Jessica. Calm down."

"Who?"

"Ow! Quit that. It's me."

The lights flicker back on.

I'm eye to eye with Jeremy Jones. "I thought I'd find you here again."

"Wha—? Sorry . . . the wardrobe was open, and I . . ." Wait a minute, was Jeremy Jones looking for me?

"No, it's closed."

"No . . ." I look. He's right. The wardrobe is closed.

But it was open. Wasn't it?

I pull the wardrobe door open. Same open space, same emus.

It looks the same. It smells different.

It smells sweet. Fresh. Like soap or potpourri.

"Are you sniffing those emus?" asks Jeremy.

"No!" *Well, not in the way you think.*

I jerk my head out of the wardrobe. And that's when I spot her turning the corner toward us, a split second before she can spot me.

I reach out and grab Jeremy, hauling him into the wardrobe with me. It's a tight squeeze for two. I pull the door almost closed.

"Shhh," I hiss at him.

"Shhh?"

"As in, be quiet," I whisper.

"As in, don't ask why you pulled me into this wardrobe?"

"As in, exactly. As in, shhh."

He doesn't shush a moment too soon. Through the crack, I watch Lavender hurry past. Throwing a quick glance over her shoulder, she ducks into a storeroom across the hall.

"Aha!" I tell Jeremy. "What do you think of that?"

"Of what? Lavender picking up an extra lightbulb for her dressing room?"

Jeremy doesn't get it.

"That's not what she's doing." I don't think.

"Then what is she doing? What are we doing?"

The wardrobe seems suddenly small, and dark, and full of Jeremy. Before a shy spasm can hit, I unlatch the door and we tumble into the hallway.

"C'mon." I signal Jeremy to be quiet as we walk toward the storeroom. Lavender has shut the door behind her, but she's still easy to hear.

"What are you doing here?" she shouts. And she has never sounded so angry.

Never.

scene 2

or one bad, belly-jumping moment, crouched low outside the door, I think Lavender has spotted me. But then I realize she's yelling at someone inside the storeroom.

"You can't stop me! Don't even try! Ah'll get out of New London. Ah'll go to Madison. Ah'll leave this state. Ah'll go to New York! Watch me!"

Who could she be talking to? Where is she going?

Jeremy is listening closely too.

"What are you *doing* here? You can't stop me! Don't even try! Ah'll get out of *New London*. Ah'll go to Madison. Ah'll leave this state. Ah'll go to New York! Watch me!"

Jeremy nods. "The first reading was better."

"Reading?"

Oh. I get it. Lavender is practicing for a role. But it's not her *Two Sisters* part. "Why would she hide out down here?"

"It's a loud scene. Maybe she's being polite."

"No, seriously. Why would she come all the way down here? She definitely doesn't want anyone to know what she's up to."

110

Jeremy looks away, and I know he's figured out the truth.

That's when I remember where Madison is.

It's the capital of Wisconsin.

Lavender is practicing for *Wisconsin Girl*. A role she thinks my sister is the main competition for.

"C'mon, Jessica. It's not a crime to rehearse."

He takes my arm, but he doesn't lead me back toward the stage. He walks to the end of the hall, pushes open a door, and we're on the lot. Sunshine momentarily dazzles.

"I'm hungry. Let's hit the commissary."

From nowhere, a flash of missing Leo charges through me. Leo would drop whatever we were doing when he got hungry. It felt so direct, so Leo, to say, "Let's eat." Even in the middle of an investigation.

The commissary is a dressed-up version of a cafeteria. The people under the hairnets are better-looking (probably because they're server-actor-producers), but the round plastic tables and chairs, the nose-wrinkling odor of mass-produced food, and the plastic trays are standard cafeteria conditions. We grab trays and throw Cokes and sandwiches onto them.

I'm relieved that Jeremy doesn't try to pay for me. (Almost totally relieved, and only one teeny, tiny bit disappointed.)

We're early for lunch so the com is pretty empty. There's only one person I recognize: Raúl, sitting alone and muttering angrily to himself.

Opposite side of the room, here I come.

Jeremy and I sit across from each other, pop our Cokes, unwrap our sandwiches, and start eating.

"Spill," he says, after a few bites.

"Where?"

"I mean, *spill*. What's going on?" He stares me down. "You're not trying to promote yourself, but you are up to something." I give my sandwich my full attention. "I thought you might be one of those gossip girls—"

My head whips up. "Selling out my sister? Jeremy, you've got me all wrong." I know I should be angry. But I feel kind of sorry for him. What is *his* family like? "I'm trying to *help* my sister."

He looks at me like the concept is deeply peculiar. And he keeps looking at me. And looking at me.

Until . . . I spill. Those cozy luau pics make me stop short of saying, "It's Lavender! Duh!" But I talk about the rest. About Project Stop Slander. About how it's got to be someone on set who is selling the stories. About the wardrobe that was open, then locked, then open. About the bead. About the hidden lock. About the text threats. About everything.

(Um . . . everything except asking Kitson if Jeremy had bought Paige's thousand-dollar bag.)

"What kind of lock is it?" Jeremy asks.

I explain that it's a gold Guardian push-button lock.

"Not much there," he says. "There are tons of Guardian locks on the set."

"I know."

Jeremy glances at me. "So was I a suspect?"

"You were." He raises an eyebrow. "But Hélène cleared you of stealing the dress, and it's hard to find a motive for the slander stuff. You don't go up for the same roles as E, and you don't need the money."

He swirls the soda in his can. "Jessica, has anyone ever told you you're a strange girl?"

"Um . . . besides Mr. Clooney, you mean?"

We burst out laughing. And then both look surprised.

A laugh like that can be like a summer storm; it's quick, but the whole temperature changes.

Jeremy says, "So do you go to a real school? With desks and blackboards and classrooms?"

I nod. "I'm going to a new school this fall."

He reads my face. "Could you look *less* excited?"

I try to smile. "It's going to be horrible. All those ri— I mean, new people. And I've never figured out how to walk into a room and just . . . start talking."

"Sounds interesting to me," says Jeremy. There's his word again. "I've missed all that stuff . . . school, bagged lunches, sports teams, mowing the lawn—"

"Mowing the lawn! I hate mowing the lawn. I used to help my dad bag the clippings. They'd get all over me, it was always a billion degrees, and after about five minutes everyone's sweaty, itchy, and stained green."

"See, I've missed out on all that." He gives the Jeremy half smile. "Anyway, you'll be great at your new school."

I can't help how quickly I look away from him.

"Jessica, there's something *else* you're not telling me?"

"No. There isn't."

There completely is!

"More mystery, huh?"

We clear our trays and head back to the set. Again, I'm reminded of Leo by the way we walk without having to say anything. Girls always seem to be talking.

When we're back on set, he says, "See ya." And heads off down the hall. Over and out.

I hurry back to the dressing room corridor, where I hear a deep, angry voice. I'm not sure I'd recognize the voice if it wasn't angry.

It's Raúl Hernandez. "You better watch where you're headed, that's all I have to say to you!" There's a pause. Then he repeats, "Watch where you're headed!"

Raúl storms out of Eva's dressing room. He doesn't seem to notice me as he stomps past. I run to Eva.

"Are you okay?"

"What?" She's lying on her couch, studying a script. "I'm fine."

She doesn't look upset. But then she didn't look upset after Mom and Dad chewed her out, either.

"I heard Raúl in here."

"Yeah."

She doesn't volunteer anything. She makes me ask: "So, what was that about?"

"Nothing."

"Nothing?"

"Do we have to get into this now? I'm trying to work through this scene."

She must read something on my face because she sighs. Puts down her script. "Okay, okay, I'll tell you."

"No, no, never mind." I'm surprised how fast the words come

out of my mouth. "You don't have to . . ." *Lie to me again*. After Chocolate, I know Eva could lie (oops—"act") right to my face and I could never tell.

E offers an olive branch. "This script is pretty good." I read the title: *Paint by Numbers*.

"Did your agent send it to you?"

"No, it's from my manicurist."

"Your manicurist knows a scriptwriter?"

"My manicurist *is* the writer."

Mani-pedi-scripty?

Paige knocks against the open door. "Hey, Eva. Just checking to see if you were going to the Spilt Sugar concert? At the Hollywood Bowl?"

E has a major crush on the lead singer.

"I'm not sure," she says. Translation: Keiko hasn't been able to score VIP tickets yet. Not without—*horror!*—paying for them.

"Oh, because I got this front-row ticket." From behind her back, Paige pulls an envelope and a small bouquet of lilacs. "Oops."

She accidentally-on-purpose drops the note. She's as much an overactor offscreen as on-.

I reach over to pick up the note: "You inspired the change in my life! Let's bring in your new year together!" As I do, I notice a sweet scent clinging to the paper. Like soap. Or potpourri.

"Just one ticket. So I guess my secret admirer will meet me there." She gives Eva a little smile. "Unless he's performing on-stage." She digs at Eva's crush. "Or unless he's been here all along."

That part she says under her breath.

It's not hard to guess that she means Jeremy.

When Paige sweeps out of the doorway, her lilacs leave their perfume in the air. And it smells like trouble.

Lilac is the new and improved scent in the emu wardrobe.

Maybe Jeremy *wasn't* looking for me near the wardrobe. Maybe he was picking up Paige's lilacs, saw me, hit the lights, and relocated the flowers (to the next-door storeroom?). Keeping his secret admirer status secret till the big birthday surprise.

Then he distracted me with lunch. And talk. And friendship.

Sure, he acted nice. But that's what he does: *act*.

"Hey, E?" My sister is still reading *Paint by Numbers*. "Is Paige's birthday coming up?" I assume that is what the admirer meant by "your new year."

"Yeah. It's in a couple of weeks. The day after the Banks party."

The party for studio head Ivan Banks and the new Mrs. Ivan is scheduled for a week from this Monday. An exclusive preview of the upcoming season will run on a Megatron screen set up on-stage, followed by eats and live music.

The Banks party is July fifteenth, so Paige's birthday is the sixteenth. Suddenly, I have a new number to add to my lock possibilities.

I race out of the dressing room and go straight to the empty corridor. The Guardian lock is exactly where I last saw it, tucked between the wall beams.

I don't ask myself why I try Paige's birthday before any of the Lavender numbers. I push in: 7-1-6.

Click!

The lock falls open.

So does my mouth.

I'm freaking—*freaking!*—about telling Jeremy everything about Project Stop Slander. But then I remember that he couldn't have taken the dress because he was with Hélène when it was stolen. But he does fit the secret admirer profile—two big clues point to him.

One, he delivered the first present himself (making up the secret admirer story when he spotted me).

Two, the gifts themselves are clues. Clues that the admirer has money, and lots of it. This guy isn't saving his burger-flipping bucks to score Fred Segal swag.

So Jeremy could be the secret admirer, but he's not the thief.

Which should make me a lot happier than it does.

scene 3

Two days later, Mom and Keiko have a meeting with the studio photographers, so it's just me and Eva making the walk to the Craft Services table. She brings her usual Krispy Kreme offering. I bring an assortment of chips and dip. Mom helped me with Abuela Lucia's recipe for the dip. The secret ingredient is a dash of buffalo-milk mozzarella.

I'm going to do some more asking around today, and I'd rather the crew was thinking about my tasty eats contribution than the fate of visiting celebrities.

In case you're wondering who this week's very special guest star is: it's *Pop Idol*'s favorite runner-up, Cal Anders. Let me tell you everything I've discovered about him this morning: He wears nice shoes. Brownish leather, possibly European. I admit that's not much of a scoop, but he seems to get hustled out of sight every time I appear.

At one point, Roman practically carries Cal past me in the hallway, and it almost sounds like one of them mutters, "I'm watching you."

Probably wasn't Cal.

You'll have to excuse Roman today. Everyone gets wound up on Fridays. It's finally time to shoot the week's episode, and a studio audience will be brought in. The energy from the audience revs up the cast and crew, with Eva sending Keiko to the theater to scout "if they look like laughers."

What surprised me the first time I saw *Two Sisters* being shot is how long it takes. With all the technical prep and styling, filming doesn't take the twenty-two minutes that you see on-screen. The audience is usually sitting for three hours. The studio keeps the drinks and snacks coming, and there is a comedian who tries to keep concert-level enthusiasm going between setups, with jokes, pranks, giveaways, and sing-alongs. Audience enthusiasm is highly important—it determines which jokes—and even which scenes—will stay or go.

The audience won't be seated till six p.m., but "shoot night" energy builds from first thing in the morning.

Shoot night or not, I can't be distracted from my mission. I've thought of some new questions for the crew: Is one of the Guardian locks missing? Did they notice anyone suspicious hanging out by the emu wardrobe?

I'll start with Lighting Guy Bob because I'm feeling brave this morning. Very brave.

Bob is circling the breakfast table and watches me approach. I can see him frowning through his white beard. I can feel him willing me not to bother him. But I keep walking toward him . . . walking toward him . . . walking toward him . . . turning left down the dressing room corridor.

Because it's a good day to investigate Lavender, too.

I pause outside her door, pretending to be tying my shoe whenever anyone appears. And wishing I hadn't worn Velcro sneakers today.

From the other side of the closed doors, I hear a woman's voice. "Mrs. Ortiz says that boundaries have been very helpful for Eva."

"Mama, what are you doing? Ignoring mah agent and taking advice from librarians?"

"Now, you be sweet, Lavender. The Cassala role is quite mature—"

Lavender interrupts. "It's challenging is what it is."

"Aw, shug . . ."

"Ah'm perfect for that role. Now tell me again what her mama said."

"She would pull Eva right out of the business before she'd consider a film like that. So Ah guess that's all taken care of."

"Ha! You don't know Eva—and neither does her mama. Ah'm the one taking care of it." Lavender's voice takes on a new softer tone. "Oh, Mama, Ah'll owe everything to you."

Wow, Lavender is bad cop and good cop in one cashmere Juicy sweater.

I'm in deep detective mode and don't notice when Jeremy appears.

"Are you trying to tie Velcro?" he asks.

I'm so surprised I almost tip over.

"Oh, sorry, Jess. I didn't mean to startle you."

Jeremy takes my hand and helps me up from my crouch.

That's when I notice the change.

The big change.

Possibly—in Hollywood—it would be considered a life change.

Everywhere else, we call it a haircut.

Jeremy went under the buzzer. The overlong blond hair is gone, replaced by a short summer cut. The bones in his face stand out. In a good way. As in Gap may even want to reshoot that ad.

We walk together, winding up in one of the large storage areas on the set; it's quiet and private.

"Lavender's mom is helping her with her evil plans," I explain. "What a great mom."

Jeremy gives me a look. "It's not an evil plan. It's her career. Actors compete for roles. Even if it's with your sister."

He's right, but something about Lavender feels wrong.

"I didn't think I'd see you today, Jessica. I've got to leave early for a satellite interview with MTV."

"From ABC to MTV with one haircut?"

"Something like that." Jeremy smiles. "Jess, I have to tell you. You were one of the inspirations for the change."

"Me?" I try not to sound too pleased. I can feel a hot blush rising up the back of my neck.

"I've been playing the same character for a few series now, and I got stuck, y'know? That guy was pretty popular, and I didn't want to risk that. Then I met you." He looks right at me. His eyes are dark and serious. I don't even breathe. "And you know how you're wildly unpopular?"

"Yes," I say softly.

Wait, what was that? Come again?

"It's so great. You don't care about being liked at all."

"Well, that's the way I am." What is he saying? Who doesn't like me? Homemade buffalo-milk mozzarella does not buy one single popularity point around here?

"If the crew had been calling me a jinx and the producer wanted to ban me from the set, I don't know that I'd just come in and take care of business the way you do."

"I take the business, all right." Suddenly I'm not feeling so well, or make that so welcome. "Um, actually, Jeremy, I think I might cut out early, too."

"All right. I just thought if you could take those risks, then so could I." I turn to head back to the dressing rooms. Maybe if I hide in Eva's room no one will even know I was here. "You know, Jess, some people might not think that being really unpopular is cool. But I do."

"Thanks."

If Jeremy said half as much, I'd like him two times better.

It's suddenly obvious just how close I am to being expelled from the set—permanently. Then I'd never be able to protect E, redeem myself with the crew, live down my past mistakes, or get fabulous free flat-iron treatments from the stylists!

scene 4

I'm lying on the couch in E's dressing room. Even if you open the door, you might not see me at first because of the way I'm lying flat with no pillow. I'm staring up at the ceiling and hoping that none of the dressers come by with costumes for E, or assistants with script changes.

Jeremy thinks I'm okay with being phenomenally unpopular.

But I'm not.

Who would be? Even the president starts harrumphing and making excuses when approval ratings fall.

At school, E always made popular look easy. And I got carried along beside her. Leo was my real best friend, but Amanda Schwab was my official best friend. She was the younger sister of Eva's official best friend. I was in Amanda's group—at the soft, squishy edge of it anyway. I'm not surprised I haven't heard from her. Not the way I am about Leo.

Eva never understood Leo.

"He's so quiet."

"Hello?" I'd say. "Have you met . . . me?"

"You? You have a million things to talk about."

With E, I have a million things to listen about. Besides, Leo wasn't quiet when he and I were hanging out. He only got tongue-tied around Eva.

I'm trying to think of an excuse to text Leo (again) when the door cracks open.

I keep quiet.

"Jess?" Eva calls.

I peek over the arm of the couch. "Hi, E."

"They're wrapping early today," Eva says. Finally, some good luck comes my way. "We should leave. Now."

"Okay, let me get my bag—"

"Leave it." Eva is already out the door, so I jump off the couch and hurry after her. She's headed away from our usual exit and winding her way between set-construction supplies, ladders, raw wood, and paint buckets. I hear her talking urgently on her cell phone to her limo driver.

"Why are we going this way?" I ask.

She clicks off her phone. "Um, no reason. Could you maybe walk faster? Or . . . run?"

I look back and see Roman appear behind us. "There she is!" he cries.

Eva is now running—in her new Jimmy Choo sandals.

One of us is in serious trouble.

I start running too. Eva pushes out through the EMERGENCY ONLY door. Alarms really do sound. I always wondered about that. She wedges a rock under the door to buy us some time as we wait for her car.

"What happened?" I ask.

Eva is still breathing hard. "Cal . . . wasn't feeling well . . . taken to hospital."

"I haven't been anywhere near him!" I could not have been responsible. "E, did you do something?"

She shakes her head. "He's at the hospital because of an allergic reaction. He's allergic to buffalo milk."

"And *I'm* being blamed?"

Eva gives me a look.

I protest. "What? He could have been exposed to buffalo milk in a hundred different ways."

Long pause.

"I think it's, like, the main ingredient in that instant creamer they use."

Longer pause.

"So, which hospital do I send flowers and an apology to?"

My wild unpopularity just got wilder.

E gets on the phone with Keiko and starts to explain every detail about what went wrong.

The limo arrives and I jump into the backseat and it roars forward.

Through the back window, I see Roman waving his fist at me. Lighting Guy Bob joins him with a gesture of his own. Eva looks as if she is talking fast.

Alone in the backseat, I start mentally composing my apology poem to Mr. Anders.

It's not going well:

> You're my favorite Idol
> almost-winner.
> Sorry my dip made you
> lose your dinner.

The drive home from the set feels strangely long—and not just because of the perpetual L.A. traffic. Maybe because it's the last time I'll be making the trip.

A slanderer, a thief, and a secret admirer might all be on the set on Monday. But I know one sister who won't.

*G*enie Wolff's column runs seven days a week. So Saturday does not equal reprieve.

The good news is that there is no photo with the Cal Anders mention in Hollywood Hype. There are limits to what even Genie will print.

The bad news is . . .

Recipe for Disaster
The ginger-haired *Pop Idol* star was left looking for ginger ale after a run-in with an Ortiz family recipe

        on the set of *Two Sisters*.
        Another Eva moment goes
        belly-up.

Eva slid a note under my door when she got back from the set last night. Cal had his stomach pumped and was back on set in time to shoot his cameo. He impressed the crew so much that they can't stand me all the more.

E doesn't come out and write the last part, but I know it's true. It's best that I not return.

I throw down the newspaper and head for some dog therapy. My bedroom now looks as if Petunia has lived there longer than I have. I like that. In fact, my whole family has kind of relaxed more now that Petunia is here—there's less walking around as if we're passing through a fancy shop.

I'm teasing Petunia with a giant rubber bone on my bed when my cell rings. I'm surprised that it's Keiko. Is she going to be the one to tell me that I'm banned from the set?

"Hi, babe. Eva wasn't answering her cell and I wanted to check in on her plan for the day."

"Hi, Keiko. She's with Janelle."

Janelle is a stylist who comes over to help E with her wardrobe.

Through Janelle, designers send clothes to Eva for free and hope she'll be photographed in them, thereby encouraging lots of her fans to go out and buy them. The fact that E can afford the clothes and few of her fans can is the funky part of the equation.

"Don't interrupt her. I was checking on the Walk of Fame photo shoot for next week, and some other things. We'll connect later."

"E told me she's going to get a massage today. Willow usually comes to the house."

Willow sets up her table outside right next to the pool, puts on some earth-sounds music, and has E feeling refreshed and relaxed in under an hour. No matter how much I splash around right next to them, the massage has remained a star perk, not a sister perk.

"Okay. Thanks."

Petunia nuzzles into my hand, panting happily.

"And Keiko . . ." There's someone I've been thinking about. "How's Chocolate? Did he get adopted?"

"Adopted?" Keiko sounds surprised. "Chocolate wasn't a stray. He was a plant."

"A plant?" Sorry, Keiko, Chocolate was definitely a member of the animal family.

"Chocolate Great Danes cost a fortune. I had to contact a top breeder. A dog like that wouldn't be hanging out at the pound."

"You *planted* a dog at the Adopt-a-Stray event?"

"In under twelve hours. With a matching collar."

Whoa, Keiko. Her hyphenate is publicist-go-to-girl. I'm glad she uses her powers for good. Or at least for Eva.

"That explains how we got a dog named Chocolate."

"Not tracking."

"It wouldn't be E's first choice. You know—because she has that terrible reaction to chocolate—instant breakout, all hyper and scattered." There's a pause on the line. It's long enough to remind me that my sister doesn't like that information getting around.

"Oh, yeah," says Keiko. Maybe she knew about E and chocolate? "You know, English bulldogs aren't usually strays, either. I wonder whose dog you got?" Panic flares through me. No one is taking my Petunia. "I hope it was that Renée Zellweger. Her publicist blackballed me from the *Vanity Fair* Oscar party." Keiko sighs. "I'm out, Jessica. Talk to you later."

Follow the lie. It's a major principle in crime solving. But how can I use it in Hollywood? Where even the *dogs* aren't what they seem.

There are little lies. Like my sister pretending to adore Krispy Kreme donuts. Like some fan-site planners pretending to be "best friends" with celebrities.

There are big lies. Like someone on the set pretending to be Eva's friend while leaking stories about her at every chance. Like Eva faxing Dad behind Mom's back.

There are lies that don't have a size, just a shadow. A stray dog that's not. Mom and Dad pretending they can be our same old parents when E's success changes everything (from the water we drink—from tap to Fiji—to how much control they have over what happens next).

There is theft. The Carolina Herrera, either sold to a secondhand shop or hanging in Lavender's bedroom.

There is spite. Hélène's lavender jersey dress. Paige's cracks about E's publicity-crashing.

There is a bad case of the creeps. Courtesy of text threats.

There are distortions of the truth, like what winds up in Genie Wolff's column.

There are secrets, like Lavender prepping for *Wisconsin Girl*. Like Paige's new admirer. (Is he Jeremy, or not?)

Even I'm not what I seem. And I'm not just talking about the secret about my school (that I'm trying to keep from even myself). I'm talking about trading Levi's for embroidered jeans, and Supercuts for a pricey salon, and wearing makeup that comes out of a stylist's silver box instead of a drugstore. And being embarrassed by my mom's old car when I used to think it was kind of cool that Dad is so good at what he does.

Petunia at my heels, I head out to the library, where I come face to face with two more people lying to each other.

The library looks as though an issue of *Vogue* exploded there. The couch alone is wearing better clothes than I ever will.

Janelle has laid out various color combinations and outfits for review. I should probably learn to tell if that top is a Stella McCartney or if that bag is a Ferragamo. Right now, I can only identify them as the blue blouse and the screamingly ugly bag. (Time to put *W* on my summer reading list—or ease into the program with *Lucky*?)

"Mrs. Ortiz, I value your opinion." Janelle's mouth is bracketed in tense lines—a clue that she is lying her couture-clad rear off. Her pants are green and brown houndstooth, topped by a flowy dark green blouse and one fierce expression. Match that with a springy Afro and a slash of glitter-green shadow over each eye, and everything about Janelle says, "Don't get between me and a trunk show."

"And I value your contribution." Mom has a matching set of tension lines, somewhat muted by her pink warm-up suit.

"Please. Let me do my job."

"Eva is still my daughter, and she's not leaving the house in either of *these*." Mom holds up two slinky purple tops. "Maybe if I sew them together, there's enough fabric for a decent shirt?"

"Mrs. Ortiz. Please. Step away from the Versace."

Mom looks around the room as if searching for strength. But she picked the wrong room.

Mom is a librarian, so this should be her favorite spot—and I think she does like the built-in bookcases, the dark wood paneling, and the high-tech computer setup. But she can't stand the books.

They're fake.

The books have pages and pictures—they're just not books we'd ever read. Some aren't even in English. They were chosen because they're old or leather or look handsome spine out.

The room is not helping.

Eva steps in smoothly. "Janelle, Lavender is going to be at the fashion shoot too. So the purple tops are out."

"Her stylist has the worst job in town," Janelle says. Then she shoots a look at Mom—like working for E has its challenges, too.

"I like the red sundress," says E tentatively.

"Yes, but . . ." Janelle spots me. And Petunia. "You have a *dog*?"

Janelle stares at little P, who is not a scary dog at all.

Petunia is friendly and bulky and warm. In her bright pink collar, the dog is off the charts on the cuteness scale.

But I can tell that all Janelle sees is a chewing/shedding/shredding/drooling machine.

Janelle starts speed-packing all the clothes. "The red sundress is a great pick, Eva. Precisely what I was thinking. It's cut to your measurements, but Hélène can tweak anything you want."

In record time, Janelle, Versace, Dior, Chanel, and Yves Saint Laurent are out the door.

Mom gives Petunia a tentative pat. "I'm starting to like this dog."

Eva smiles at me. I'm about to apologize to her about Cal again, but she raises her hand before I can speak. "I know, I know. It's been a rough week. But I have a great idea for how we can both relax."

I'm thinking: soothing massage.

It's easy to ignore the little warning voice whispering, "E is full of surprises."

$\mathcal{F}$ red Segal Beauty in Santa Monica. The palace of pampering, and Eva leads me right to the spa. Mom is getting her nails done at the salon.

I can't believe how understanding E is being about my bad luck—I know Mom has been after her to keep me involved and get me out of the house—but still, I was expecting to get told off, not hauled off to a beauty mecca.

My sister and I share a treatment room, separated by a curtain. Eva explained that Willow wasn't able to fit her in today (something about Penelope and Salma), so she thought Fred Segal would be a great treat.

Tranquil music plays. I lie with my towel draped over my back, facedown on the cushioned massage table. My body therapist, Uta, seems like a lovely person.

Smiling, pleasant, thoughtful.

There is no outward sign that she has aggression issues. Until she proceeds to work out on my back.

Yowch!

How does a tiny woman have such strong hands?

"I feel that you are fighting me," says Uta, concerned. "Maybe this kind of massage—"

"No, no. I'm fine." I grit my teeth. There is no way I'm messing up a massage! I'm going to relax if it kills me.

"Is this your first massage?" she asks.

Who are you? Tennis Neighbor? "No, I get massages all the time. Constantly."

"Deep tissue?"

"Yes. Sure."

The next sixty minutes feel like six hundred. Through the curtain, I hear Eva telling her masseuse what a fantastic job she's doing. How she'll be sure to ask for her when she comes again.

Uta tries to talk with me, but my teeth are clenched together so I can't respond. Time passes and either Uta lightens up or I lose consciousness—at any rate the massage is over.

I hear Eva thanking her therapist. "Energy balancing was the way to go. I feel so much better."

The curtain parts and Eva steps through, chirpy as a robin. I peel myself off the table. In Uta's defense, I'm certainly not tense. I would need to have a shred of muscle mass remaining to be tense.

I thank Uta, and Eva and I head back to the changing room, where I see a description of the massages posted.

Eva's:

Energy-balancing massage: through light contact, therapist re-aligns your energy field. Helping energy within you flow properly to bodily systems.

And mine:

Deep tissue: designed to benefit overuse in muscle. Begins like firm Swedish until tissue is broken down enough to begin deep penetrating work.

That's when I realize it wasn't Uta working out her aggression issues—it was my sister!

"How was your massage?" Eva asks.

"It was fantastic! I have never felt so good. The next time you get a massage, be sure to ask for deep tissue."

"Really?"

"Really. Uta said something about how it's the only massage that masseuses themselves ever go for. All the other energy, hot stones, balancing stuff—it's kind of a joke."

I love my sister, and I know she loves me. But when you live with someone and you stomp around in each other's business, steam has got to be blown off somehow.

"Steam room?" Eva suggests.

"Great idea."

We meet Mom at the salon.

There is something I want to check out in the shopping section of Fred Segal. But I don't want Mom and Eva to suspect what I'm up to.

"Can we look around the store before we go?" I ask casually.

"Sounds good," says Eva.

"Well, I'm not sure . . . ," says Mom, checking her watch.

E jumps in. "My session with Janelle was not quite—"

Mom cuts her off with a look. "Fifteen minutes," she says sharply. "Meet me on Broadway in fifteen minutes."

I'm already gone.

140

Fred Segal is arranged as a collection of boutiques, and each boutique has its own name: FS Apothia for cosmetics, FS Lifesize for children's clothes, FS Couture, FS Feeling, FS Sparkle. I'm headed to FS Sparkle.

There is a stylish, twenty-something redhead behind the counter. I start circling the jewelry display. "May I help you?" she asks.

Usually even a little lie makes me tense up, but post-Uta, I barely even bat an eye. "I collect sunflower jewelry and heard that you might have some pieces here?"

"Oh, yes. Sunflowers are popular right now." She selects a necklace with a sunflower pendant, a bracelet, and a familiar pair of earrings.

"Those earrings are gorgeous. How much do they cost?"

"They're nine hundred."

My first thought is nine hundred *what*? Then I realize she means nine hundred dollars. Claire's at the mall never looked like such a bargain.

She must see the look on my face because she explains, "The diamonds are almost half a carat, and the flower is fourteen-carat gold, inlaid with topaz."

"They are pretty. Um . . . I heard Jeremy Jones was shopping here this week? Did you get to meet him?"

She starts putting the pieces back. "No, I hadn't heard that. But we get celebrities in here regularly. It wouldn't surprise me." She gives me a smile. "I heard Eva Ortiz was at the spa, if you're a *Two Sisters* fan."

Even now, I get surprised when people refer to Eva as a star. Sometimes all I can think is: Eva? She's just my sister.

"Thanks," I say. And I mean it. She knew I was about $890 short on affording those earrings, but she was still nice about it without knowing whose sister I am.

"And I passed Genie Wolff—the gossip columnist—over in the shoe section right before I came on my shift. You might still catch her."

I head out of Sparkle in a hurry. My fifteen minutes are almost up, but I can't resist a chance to see Genie Wolff in person. Maybe I'll even think of some way to talk to her. To explain.

I'm almost jogging into the shoe section when I see the face that I've previously seen only in smudgy half-inch black-and-white next to her column.

But it isn't Genie who has me staring in horror. It's who she's with.

*G*enie Wolff's photo doesn't do her justice.

In person, her eyes are much more like evil blue blazes. She fires a glare at the shoe assistant and starts tossing around boxes of Dolce & Gabbana sandals and slingbacks.

The salesperson collects the boxes, and Genie returns to her deep, private consultation with . . . Keiko!

It's an intense conversation. And why not? They speak the same language.

Is Keiko looking to trade information on Eva to get herself a better position with someone else? Genie Wolff has tons of connections in publicity, if Keiko is looking for a new job.

I go through the history in my head.

Keiko was on the scene for the Ashton and the Clooney incidents. In the chaos, she could have quietly snapped off some pics with her cell phone camera. She knows my phone number if she wanted to send me threatening text messages. She overheard at least part of the *Angst* conversation. She wasn't on set when Cal

Anders became ill, but Eva told her all about it. And that was the one time when a Genie article didn't have a picture.

And then there's the missing dress. I'm not sure the leaker and the Carolina Herrera thief are the same person, but the day the dress was stolen, Keiko was on the set early. She had told Mom she was trying to find out who had snapped the Clooney pic that appeared in Hype. Maybe Keiko has suddenly gotten desperate for cash? If she likes shopping at Fred Segal (where a tank top can set you back $150), she might be desperate for dollars.

And then, there's today. Right now.

I was the one to tell Keiko that Eva would be at the house. So it was safe to come out in public. To have a merry little shoe-shopping trip to Santa Monica.

I'm bothered by three questions:

By ignoring the shoe-licker, did I overlook the key player?

The pieces fit, but where is the proof?

Do I have enough to go to my mom or Eva?

I hurry out of the shoe department—any thought of confronting Genie abandoned—through the FS boutiques and out onto the street.

I face another bad scene.

The Nissan is double-parked on Broadway. And it's surrounded by autograph seekers. Eva is signing as quickly as she can, but I can see that her smile is forced. The squeeze of the human knot around her is uncomfortable. Mom is at her side, arms out, trying to create breathing space.

Crowds have a personality different from any of the people in them. And this crowd is pushy.

"Sign this!"

"Are you and Jeremy dating?"

"Look at my camera!"

I get the vibe that the people aren't exactly *Two Sisters* fans, but the kind of people that grab at something that's free. Just because someone else might want it.

Mom sees me. And she's M-A-D mad.

She doesn't say a word about me being late. She opens the door and half-pushes Eva into the Nissan. She takes me by the arm and drags me around to her side of the car, where I jump into the backseat. Mom gets behind the wheel.

Fans are still pressing closer to the car, but Mom guns the motor.

"Mom," Eva says between her teeth. "I have to be nice."

"I don't."

The Nissan peels out. I don't know what Dad put under the hood of this thing, but it can *go*.

"Sorry I was late, E." I don't even try to talk to Mom.

"We were hanging in the car, and this little girl asked for an autograph. When I got out of the car, a few more people came by. And then . . . you know. I hope we didn't run over anyone's feet." Eva looks back to throw me a grin. "Don't tell Keiko about this one."

I gulp back a lump in my throat. "I won't."

Act
IV

I have to remind my dad, journalists—no matter how many
cigars they smoke with you—are not your friends,
so don't talk to them.

—CAMERON DIAZ

*I*t's with a feeling of eerie inevitability that I open to Hollywood Hype to read another damaging article about my sister. Sunday has just become a day of unrest at the Ortiz house.

Breakout Latina—or Fakeout?

Eva Ortiz has been named Breakout Star by the Latino Awards—but does she qualify? It seems even the star herself isn't sure. Inside sources confirm that the services of cultural instructor Raúl Hernandez have been employed to teach Eva "how to be Latina." When you need classes in how to eat an enchilada, Hollywood Hype wonders if

an award is in order—or re-
medial Spanish?

The accompanying photo is of Raúl Hernandez. I almost don't recognize him because he's smiling and dressed in a trim blazer and collared shirt. The photo is as polished as a head shot.

We are Latino—but are we Latino enough?

It wasn't a secret that Eva was meeting with Raúl. Anyone who wanted to know could have found out what her lessons were about. With the Latino Awards coming up, Eva's agent thought E should be better informed, and Raúl was hired to teach local history and some Spanish.

Eva's team isn't taking this story lying down. There's already a group gathered in the living room: Eva, Mom, Dad, Raúl Hernandez, Keiko, Eva's agent Paula Joseph (aka Power Paula), and a couple of Paula's assistants. If you've seen Paula power walking in her power suit while power negotiating on her solar-powered cell phone, you'll know where the name comes from. I get a power headache being around her.

And when Paula's around, there's usually a power struggle with Mom. Mom and Paula used to have a great relationship, but as Eva's star began to rise, so did the tension between them. They want to pull Eva in opposite directions: bigger and busier on Paula's side; smaller and slower on Mom's side. Paula tries to downplay her interaction with Mom to keep the peace at Eva, Inc. The tension has meant that Keiko winds up in the middle, getting more involved than your average publicist.

I used to feel sorry for her.

Of course, Keiko knew all about Raúl. The lessons have been going on for weeks; I guess she was waiting for a slow news day to sell it to Genie. Maybe it paid for a new pair of shoes.

I enter the living room. I've got to tell Eva that Keiko is the slanderer. It can't wait. "E?"

My sister turns and for a moment I can feel the intensity she is bringing to the situation. She forcibly relaxes and smiles at me. "It's all right, Jess. Don't worry."

Power Paula shoots me a hard look and keeps on talking strategy. I sit quietly in the back, waiting for a chance to get to E.

"I'm sorry that—" begins Raúl, dragging a hand through his gray hair.

Paula cuts him off. "Your time will come, Mr. Hernandez." She turns to Eva. "Look, we've got a real chance to strike back at Genie on this, but we want to do it right. Anytime you get into questions about ethnicity, there's going to be controversy. We want to be smart."

Here's the history. Our last name is Ortiz. We're mostly Latino, except that Mom is part Irish. No, my sister doesn't understand much Spanish, outside the Billy's Burrito Bar menu. Yes, my sister's middle name is Colleen, after Grammy O'Malley. Why does that seem like it should be a secret now?

Mom is agitated. "I told you, Keiko. We should have fought back against the very first sign of this bullying. This *libel*. Back when the Kutcher article was full of lies."

I know what Mom is saying, but sometimes Eva, Inc., uses its own lies—adopting "stray dogs;" "denying" Jeremy dating rumors. The edges get blurry sometimes. And then they get crossed.

Keiko twists her hands in her lap.

Power Paula answers, "This is a better platform." She looks at Mom and Dad. "Susan, Rob—*Roberto*—we need you here."

Mom looks surprised. "You do?"

"Yes. Right here. *Rightthisveryhere.*" She pauses. "But perhaps in the kitchen?"

It's Paula's power play.

And one she's wanted to make for a while: *Clear out, Mamá. There's work to be done.*

Dad doesn't say anything. He stands up. And it's not even that he's a big man. It's just that he can seem barely restrained at times. This is one of those times.

I don't know which way Mom is going to jump. She's not afraid to take on Paula, and she knows that Dad will back her up. But then there's Eva.

Eva looks as if even a week on Uta's table wouldn't unwind her. Eva, tense and worried. Eva, Paula's trump card.

"Rob, it looks like Eva could use a beverage." Mom nods at Dad. He gives Paula a long look and follows Mom out of the room.

I'm not planning to leave the living room. I'm quiet in the corner, representing the family.

Then Keiko says, "I picked up some special teas this morning! I'll go make some for Eva and Paula."

And, of course, I have to follow. Keiko is wearing a silky bright red dress pulled in by a drawstring waist. Her white hair is extra-choppy-spiky today, so from behind she looks like a lit candle. But maybe that's because I'm wondering who she is going to burn next.

Mom and Dad are in the kitchen, looking calmer and talking quietly. ". . . we'll let Paula run this. It's the kind of thing she does. We can make the big decisions later. When it's just us."

Dad nods and heads out to the patio.

Mom gives me a smile that seems mostly real. "Paula decided to hold a press conference here this morning. Good thing we live in a Spanish-style *casa*." Mom looks at Keiko. "Keiko was able to get chairs and a podium delivered in under an hour. There's not much she can't do."

There's not much she *won't* do. Big difference.

Keiko smiles. She makes herself at home, putting a Tea Café thermos in the microwave and rooting around in our cabinets for teacups. The ones she finds are decorated with elegant scrolls and sit on matching saucers. Mom and I exchange surprised glances. We've never seen them before. The Beverly Hills home designers are thorough: *moneymoneymoney*.

Mom nods at me. "Jessica, will you help Dad review the setup outside? He wanted to make sure the microphone was working. You know how he is."

"Sure, Mom."

But I don't move. My eyes are on Keiko. She's pulling packets out of the Tea Café bag. Of course she knows how Eva and Paula like their tea. Not too hot, just nicely warm. No milk for either. A packet of Equal for Paula, and for Eva . . . Keiko half-turns so that her back is to Mom and me. It's only by straining my neck that I see her drop two squares into E's tea.

Brown squares.

Chocolate squares?

Is Keiko setting my sister up to break out and break down at her big press conference? Genie would pay for that kind of story—and be relieved to have the press distracted from her wobbly Fakina scoop.

Keiko sets the cups and saucers on a silver tray.

She's about to walk right past me when I decide—sometimes it's a good thing to have a reputation as a one-person disaster area.

I jump up, knocking the tray. Tea and posh cups go tumbling. Green tea splashes against Keiko's red dress.

"Hey!" Keiko gives me a furious look.

"Sorry." I reach down to pick up the cups. I'm trying to see if a lump of chocolate is still visible.

Nothing. The evidence melted away.

Mom rushes over to apologize. "Come with me to the laundry room and we'll get some spot cleaner on that." Then she turns to me and squeezes her eyes shut. "Please, Jessica. Go outside."

"But Mom, I have to tell you—"

"Out. Side." It's two words only when Mom is angry. Very angry. In-no-mood-to-listen-to-publicist-conspiracy-theory angry.

Keiko follows Mom, jabbing me with another angry glance. Because I spoiled her dress . . . or her plan?

So I head outside and see a new arrival: Steve, the *Two Sisters* hairstylist. He's more visibly worked up than anyone else. He's got a big black carpetbag open on the patio table and is searching frantically.

"Hi, Steve."

"Jessica." He barely glances up. "Can you believe they're asking so much of me?"

Blow-drying? Styling?

"They want me to create a whole new look for Eva *right now*." He pulls brushes, a sleek black blow-dryer, and a flat iron out of the bag. "Don't they know I have to live with an idea for my actors? We're talking about a new signature look for Eva—that can't be rushed."

"Why now?" I ask. Hair seems trivial considering what's going on.

"They're thinking that since Jeremy got attention with his haircut, if I whip up something fabulous, it will distract from the Latina-Fakina thing."

"Steve," calls Power Paula. "We're ready for you."

Panic touches Steve's eyes. Then his fingers close on . . . a plain black comb. "Got it." He looks at me. "It's my lucky comb. Comby."

"Comby?" That's why few hairstylists are stylist-screenwriters.

A look of determination has come over Steve's face. He reaches for his supplies bag as if it's a bomb-detonating tool kit and the countdown has begun.

Dad doesn't want my help setting up the microphone, but I try to stay useful. I put away the pictures of the Irish part of the family and place the Ortizes center stage throughout the hallway where the press will enter. I hope Grammy Colleen doesn't find out.

And every second, I keep an eye out for when I can get a moment with Eva. Away from Keiko.

The moment doesn't come. A handful of reporters arrive—some print, a couple of TV. Paula, Keiko, and Raúl are prepping Eva while Steve works on her hair. Mary from the makeup department has also arrived to assist.

"Pinch your cheeks," says Mary.

"Face the camera," says Paula.

"Hold your head still," says Steve.

"Watch for me," says Raúl.

"Don't forget to smile!" says Keiko.

They lead Eva out of the living room. I make my move, barreling between Paula's assistants to get beside my sister.

"E, I need a minute."

Paula gives me a glare that causes the ficus plants behind me to wither and droop. I can't hold her look, but I don't back away from Eva either. "It can't wait."

E steps out of the cluster. "What is it?"

I'm not going to be able to get her any farther away from the group. So I press close to her shiny hair and whisper into her ear: "It's Keiko. She's responsible for all of this. Everything that's happening."

My sister looks right at me and says the last two words I expect to come out of her mouth: "I know."

Then she goes straight to the microphone.

scene 2

*O*n our patio, the reporters sit on folding chairs in front of the black, gleaming podium. The chairs aren't cheap church bingo chairs, but wedding-chair white with bows that say Hello/*Hola* wrapped around them. Keiko is good at what she does. Unfortunately.

The reporters have their recorders and notepads out. A couple of photographers mill about, talking to the few camera crews that have made the trip.

Power Paula had considered introducing Eva, or inviting Jeremy, Lavender, and Paige to amp the star wattage. But Paula ultimately decided that Eva walking straight out the door of her home and taking the podium alone might have more impact. So that's what my sister does.

Steve has done good work. Eva's dark brown hair now has a rich henna tint and has been blown out straight and shortened to her shoulder blades. The color brings out the gold in her eyes. Normally, *TeenStyle* would devote a two-page review to a cut like that . . . but today I can see the reporters won't be distracted so easily.

I take a seat between Power Paula and Keiko.

Eva begins to move through her speech. She refers to note cards, which surprises me because she has an amazing memory, but then she's only had a few hours to learn the speech.

"I am a proud Latina. And a proud American. My heritage, like that of our city, makes little sense when one tries to separate one element from the other."

She goes on to say how L.A. is a mix of two cultures, benefiting everything from architecture to food, music, and fashion, and that her desire to learn more about her culture makes her a model for American Latinas. It sounds book reportish, but you get the idea.

Then Eva veers off in a new direction. I don't understand a word of what she's saying. Literally.

Because my sister is speaking in nonstop Spanish!

I'm impressed. Good for Eva.

I exhale. A short speech, a photo op with henna hair, we're home free.

I look around at the press corps. I can feel that E's charm is working on them, but that they're not convinced. GOSSIP COLUMNIST OVERSTATES CASE is not much of a headline compared to TV STAR FAKES HERITAGE TO GRAB AWARD. The reporters aren't going to back off yet.

Keiko says, "Here we go!" under her breath; she even whispers with exclamation points. Then she moves to the mike and announces that Eva will now take questions.

Keiko scans the audience. I see her homing in on a sharp-eyed commentator from TV Español. *Not him!* I want to shout.

But of course Keiko nods at him. "The reporter from TV Español?"

His question may be perfectly straightforward, but it's nonsensical to me: It's in Spanish. All eyes flip back to Eva, who returns slowly to the mike.

Why did she ever speak in Spanish?

Eva opened herself up for this. She should have admitted that she has a lot to learn about Latino culture and left it at that. (Not that Eva would go for any plan that has the word *admit* in it. She's a little Martha Stewart like that.)

I can't watch.

This is going to be awful.

Eva is going to . . . speak fluent Spanish?

For all I know, she may be standing there making sounds up, but from the way the guy from TV Español is nodding along, I don't think so. For a minute, I guess someone is feeding Eva answers through an earpiece, but her hair is tucked back around her ears—no earpiece. As she's speaking, E comes around in front of the podium. She's making it clear that she's not hooked up to any kind of listening device.

Next Eva takes another question—and answers it in Spanish. Then another one. Whatever that answer was, people are really nodding now.

A reporter from *TeenStyle* raises her hand. "I hope you're still taking questions in English?" she jokes. The crowd laughs—a big, we-never-doubted-you-for-a-minute laugh. "Because I'd love to ask about your new haircut."

It is then that I declare total victory for Eva. She not only took on Genie's cracks, but she also answered with grace. Eva poses with the representative from the Latino Awards and signs autographs.

The reporters disperse quickly, grabbing some of the cheese empanadas that Mali quickly put together. An Eva disaster would have been a bigger story; her triumph cuts down on her column space.

The camera vans are pulling away when Tennis Neighbor walks by. She gives our house a look like a press conference is the tackiest thing that's ever happened to her neighborhood. She might be right, but if she keeps up those snotty glares, I'm going to talk Dad into putting broken cars on blocks, and plaid couches on the lawn.

Eva's "people"—agent, publicist, assistants—start to head out as well. Keiko lets Mom know that she would "like to help clean up!" Then she leaves immediately. I help Dad fold up the chairs and stack them for the rental company.

When I head inside, I find Eva alone in the kitchen. She's reading *Variety* and munching on celery stalks. (Her trainer confirmed that when you eat celery you burn more calories than you consume.)

I have to know: "E, did you learn Spanish in one morning?"

"How likely is that?" she asks.

I don't know what to say. It's foolish to underestimate Eva.

She nudges my shoulder, as if it's a joke I should be in on. "I memorized it," she says. "You know, phonetically. I memorized the sounds. I didn't know exactly what I was saying."

"But how did you answer the questions?"

"Did you see how Mr. Hernandez was seated in the front row?" asks Eva. "We rehearsed a bunch of answers this morning and coded them one through ten. After the question, he would press his fingers against his face—you know, give me the signal as to which answer to give."

"You memorized all that Spanish *phonetically*?"

"It's what I do. Memorize. Act," she says with a shrug. "Before he learned English, Antonio Banderas memorized his *Mambo Kings* lines that way."

Ay, caramba.

"That's why I used note cards for the English part. Create a greater contrast with the 'spontaneous' responses."

I don't know whether to be disappointed or impressed. It's one thing to learn a foreign language overnight (sleeping on a Spanish dictionary does *not* work). It's something else to put on a show in a foreign language and score rave reviews. Is that the difference between a student and a star?

Eva winks at me, and suddenly I realize it wasn't speaking Spanish that showed her Latina roots, it was pulling off her plan *con sabor*—with flavor!

"Besides, I thought you knew about it. Your whole 'Keiko is responsible' speech."

"Keiko?" I try not to look as confused as I feel.

"Yeah. She came up with the whole idea. First she convinced Genie Wolff to run that Petunia story; then she tracked Genie all over town—even *shoe shopping*—to try to kill the Latina story. When Genie wouldn't drop it, Keiko came up with the 'Spanish answers' idea. It's based on an old magic act her aunt used to do."

I'm realizing something. Slowly.

"E, our trip to Fred Segal . . . did we go there because Genie and Keiko were there?"

Eva brightens. Like she's impressed that I figured the plan

out. Not that she got busted dressing up a business trip as a family holiday.

"I wanted to take you and Mom out for something special. But yeah, Keiko and I thought it might make a difference if I met with Genie myself. Didn't happen, though. Keiko's read was that Genie wouldn't appreciate an ambush and I'd lose whatever star standing I have with her."

"Keiko really came through for you."

"Absolutely. I can always use someone like the Key." Now she's even got a nickname. "Who would have thought she'd be the one to save the day?"

Honestly?

Not me.

I had cast Keiko as the villain. Not the hero.

The only good news is that the apology poem comes to me pretty quickly. (Of course I don't mention that to the preju-diced eye, two lumps of brown sugar had looked like chocolate squares.)

Keiko, thanks for all you do
To keep our Eva's image true.

You always get the job done
A publicist army, all in one.
So sorry for the tea spill
Please do send the cleaning bill.

My poem complete, I know what I have to do next.
Or make that what I have to *not* do.

I t's a new morning. Eva is going to the set, but I'm not going with her. Today I play with Petunia and watch TV. There's nothing on. I watch for six hours.

T oday I teach Petunia to almost sit up. A soap opera called *Doctors* premieres. I decide that I will watch it every day that it airs and perhaps earn an invitation to its twenty-fifth anniversary. Goals are important.

166

Today I teach Petunia to eat a dog biscuit (she pretty much knew that, but I'm trying to show some progress). On *Doctors,* Dr. Stan and Dr. Sharon get into a screaming fight about the conjoined baby triplets that they're separating.

Today I teach Petunia to roll over—when she feels like it. Dr. Stan and Dr. Sharon sue each other over the tragic triplets.

Today I give Petunia the day off from her grueling training regime. Dr. Stan and Dr. Sharon get married. The triplets are now separated, sixteen years old, and hot.

Today Petunia discovers a new chew toy: E's Lacoste polo shirt. I hide the discovery under Petunia's bed.

It's Saturday, so I can only guess about the teaser for next week's *Doctors*. Dr. Stan and Dr. Sharon are haunted by the ghost of the fourth triplet.

*M*om comes in to make sure I'm not wasting all my time in front of the television.

"What? You think I'm zoned in front of soaps and *E! True Hollywood Story* all week? Maybe I've been in here reading, playing with Petunia, meditating."

I managed to snap off the TV *seconds* before Mom came into the room.

Mom takes a look at my face, then reaches over to feel the back of the TV. It's smoking hot. A million hours of operation will do that, I guess.

Again, why did E have to hog all the acting ability in the family?

Mom kicks me out. Out to the pool, that is.

Her parting words: "If you want to talk, Jessica, or show me any of your poems, I'll be in the kitchen."

Spooky. How does she know when I've written a new poem? "There are no poems, Mom."

Here's another one she'll never see.

> *People on E's payroll*
> *Everywhere she looks*
> *Masseuse, trainer, publicist,*

Accountant for the books.
Agent taking 10 percent,
A maid who cleans and cooks.

Money changes everything—
Even Mom and Dad and me.
Look for the silver lining:
At least the clothes are free.

So when the press turns bad
Watch everyone get bent.
Their panic says, "You're not set here;
You're just the folks who rent."

I lounge on a chair by the pool, Petunia at my feet. I'm trying to
decide if I can cheat the "even" in line eight to an "ev'n," when
something terrible happens.

Something awful.

Dreadful.

B-A-D. Bad.

I take a nap.

But that's not the awful, dreadful, B-A-D, bad part. That part is the dream.

In the dream, it's one month ago, a sunny June day, and I stop by to get an early look at my new school. And for it to get a look at me.

I went to public school in Anaheim, but here I'll be attending a high-priced, Catholic academy. In the dream, I'm walking the grounds with Jeremy Jones. Whitewashed villas are set on rolling lawns; picnic tables wait under white and blue striped tents for lunch; a bell tolls from the small central chapel.

Jeremy turns to me and says, "Jessica, is there something *else* you're not telling me?"

I shake my head, but then Jeremy disappears and I'm with Sister Carmen, standing in front of my classmates-to-be. "Our very special guest today is Jessica Ortiz. Jessica, could you tell us a little bit about yourself, please?"

Those words make everything I've ever known about myself fly out of my head. For a minute, I even blank on my own middle name. Lucia. Jessica Lucia. Jessica Lucia, breathe deeply. Jessica Lucia, say something!

You, I'm confident, would be above trying to leverage your sister's celebrity to make friends. And I am too.

Or at least, I start off above it and kind of slowly sink.

"I'm Jessica. From Anaheim." The eyes of my future classmates are glazing over—and I don't need to tell you how important the first impression at a new school is, do I? So I decide to drop one small Hollywood mention. I won't bring up E directly, but maybe with the last name Ortiz, and an offhand movie remark . . . my new hoped-for friends might make the sister-to-star connection? I manage to mumble: "And last summer . . . I was an extra in a movie." (The movie was a big blockbuster that Eva had a tiny role in; my role as back-of-head-on-the-right was even tinier.)

The reaction I hope for: we see an interesting future friend!

The reaction I fear: we smell a trying-too-hard poseur!

The reaction I get: horrified silence. One of the girls in the front row gently moves her fingers over the small cross that hangs from her neck.

"Ahem . . . ," says Sister Carmen, looking at me oddly. "That is . . . oh, my." She hustles me out of the room with surprising speed for someone in sensible shoes.

I'm feeling anxious and disoriented. "Sister Carmen, was being an extra in a movie the wrong kind of thing to mention?"

"Extra?" Sister Carmen blinks. "My girl, it sounded like you said you'd been in an *X-rated* movie."

I wake up. My stomach is clenched. The dream is over, but the nightmare is real. This dream was a memory—of exactly how I introduced myself to my classmates at Holy Sisters Academy on my brief visit.

I didn't tell Mom or E or anyone about what happened. It's been my secret. Even in my own mind, I locked the story behind a secret door. Till it broke down the door into my dream.

Stupid door.

Now I admit it: Maybe a part of Project Stop Slander was a distraction from the whole HSA disaster. That doesn't mean I didn't want to help Eva.

I did and I do. It was just such a surprise to see that the show I thought I was in (*Ortiz Family Works Together!*) was so different from the one everyone else was watching (*Eva's Sister Needs to Get Her Own Life!*).

Mali comes out bearing a cup of pink lemonade. "Crushed ice, not cubes."

She knows how I like my lemonade, which is more than I know about her.

"It is good to be out in the sun, yes? Even the soft U.S.A. sun?"

"Mali has a stronger sun?"

"Yes, more golden light. Mali is rich in sun."

I had Googled Mali and found out it is one of the poorest nations in Africa, largely desert, and with a political history of corruption and warfare. Can you miss a place like that, even if it's home? I look at Mali's face and know the answer.

"You must miss it."

"Yes." Her face is calm. "I must." She walks back to the house, earrings swaying under her headdress.

Our conversation feels like a minitrip to brat camp.

I'm overdue to take my life in a new direction—where I stop dressing my dog in funny hats and meet some non-*Doctors* people. It's time to make a crucial decision about my future.

I know I'm a little young for it, but I've decided to retire. I'm leaving the detective business.

After Eva's instant Spanish display, aided by Keiko the Capable, I can't believe that my sister could ever need my help. Disasters bounce off Eva like bullets off Superman. Trouble is allergic to her. She's protected by some crazy karma.

A tap on my sun hat interrupts my thoughts.

"Jess, I need your help. And I need it badly."

I look up at my sister. After everything that has happened, I know an act when I see it.

Don't I?

I squint up at Eva. She needs *me*? "That's hard to believe, Señorita."

Eva sits on the lounge chair, facing me. "I did something that I possibly—maybe—should not have done."

"Don't tell me: You're not Latina after all. You're Eva O'Rourke."

"Jessica, I'm serious." Eva looks serious—as serious as she looked in the "Polly's Last Cracker" episode.

And then I notice two things: the crinkle of wrapper when Eva fidgets on the edge of the seat, and a slight smell of chocolate. Is my sister back on the bean—the *cocoa* bean? I see the dark brown of an M&M wrapper peeking from her jean pocket. My sister's face is already looking . . . bumpier.

This is serious.

What could have driven her to the world of sugary goodness?

Not looking at me, Eva admits: "Last week, I made an audition reel for the Sophie Cassala film."

"What?"

"You know, a recording of my performance to send Ms. Cassala."

"Mom said you couldn't audition, and you decided that meant you couldn't audition *in person,* but that sending a DVD was okay?"

"Once I got the job, Mom would realize that the role was *not* too adult. She'd never have to know about the audition. She'd assume I was hired off my *Two Sisters* work, right? Sophie Cassala offering me a job is something Mom would have to take seriously." I look at Eva skeptically. My sister is not dumb, but she can exercise selective judgment when it suits her. "It's only a matter of time before Mom realizes that I'm perfect for the role of a Wisconsin runaway, pregnant and strung out."

I can't imagine how long a time that would be.

"So what's the problem?" I can see about a hundred problems myself, but I couldn't begin to guess what Eva thinks the problem is.

"The DVD is missing."

"And you're afraid it will show up in the press somewhere? Make you look like you're a pregnant Wisconsan?"

"Jess, I'm serious. If this DVD gets out, it's all over for me."

"E, I couldn't worry about you if I wanted to! You're like that Rumpelstiltskin princess. You can spin gold out of straw."

"Yes. But I can't spin Mom."

Good point.

"Jess, will you help me? That DVD was made after Steve dyed my hair—and Mom knows that's *after* she forbade me to pursue this."

I don't want you to think less of Eva for this. Haven't you ever reached for that extra cheese fry when you were already full? Or wondered where that bag of chips went before you remembered that you ate it? Eva's appetite is what gets her in trouble. I know she crossed a line here. But she's my sister, so all I have to say to her at a time like this is: "Where's the last place you remember seeing the DVD?"

Eva sighs. "I worked with Rocky on it. He directed it and was going to edit it for me."

"But instead . . ."

"He gave it to Lavender."

"*What!* Why would he do that?"

Eva allows a small crease to appear on her forehead. "Because her accent sounds so honey-chile sweet. Because she told him she was such a fan of my work, she couldn't wait to see it, and that I was her best friend and wouldn't mind. And mainly . . . because people do what she wants them to do."

"Did you ask Lavender for it?"

"She said she 'lost' it. She acted sorry."

Acted.

It's still hard to worry about Eva. "Even if Lavender gives it to Genie Wolff, with your luck, Mom would never see the column or any press about it."

"That's why I don't think it will show up in the column. If I was Lavender—not that I can *imagine* what she thinks like—I'd courier it to Mom personally."

"I can watch the deliveries at home."

"Then she'll have the DVD played at the big Banks party in two days. Mom won't miss that."

"The party or the audition?"

"Exactly."

Oh dear. My retirement is brief.

I can't stop myself from asking: "But what about Keiko? Can't she help?"

"Key is amazing. No doubt. But I don't want anything to get back to Mom. With Keiko, I couldn't be sure. . . ." She trails off. "So will you help me?"

Eva and Jessica versus Mom and Dad. That story goes back

beyond Beverly Hills. Back to sneaking an extra half hour of Saturday morning cartoons. To taping up a torn Berenstain Bears book at the library. To splitting a forbidden Twinkie from the kitchen. Back through my whole life.

E knew the answer before she asked the question. I nod and she gives me a quick hug. "Thanks, Jess."

Mom calls from the kitchen. "Eva, Keiko called. The limo is on its way."

"Okay, Mom," E calls back. She turns to me. "There's a photo shoot for the cast at the Walk of Fame."

Eva gives me her superstar smile, and it's instantly hard to believe that she really is worried about the DVD. Maybe she came up with all this to get me out of the house? Then I spot the evidence. A small trail of M&M's falls from her lowriders.

That DVD could plunge my family back to the "little" house. And as much as Beverly Hills can sometimes drive me crazy, we've given up too much to let that happen.

I return Eva's smile. "I'm there."

*N*othing is going to distract me from my sleuthing.

Except for true love.

"Woof!"

"Petunia! Come back!" Petunia and I are racing around in the yard, waiting for the *Two Sisters* limo to arrive.

Eva has to stay fresh and prepped inside, but I can get as dirty and scratched up as I like. When the limo pulls up, I'm on all fours tugging with both hands on a pink rubber bone with my bulldog. Covered in grime. Grass in my hair. Laughing like a loon.

Not the ideal reintroduction to Jeremy Jones.

Who of course looks camera-ready in black jeans and a faded band T-shirt.

"Hi, Jessica. Haven't seen you around lately."

I can't quite meet his eye. "Yeah. I had some *Doctors* business." I drop the chew toy, wiping slobber on my jeans. "I wasn't expecting you."

Obviously.

"Since we're shooting at the Walk of Fame, there are going to be people watching us arrive," Jeremy explains. "The publicists thought the show would look friendlier if the cast arrived together."

"So Paige and Lavender?"

Jeremy points back at the limo. "Don't want to get out of the car."

Not especially friendly.

"Eva really has a dog?" Jeremy squats next to me to rub Petunia in the soft spot behind her ears. "It's hard to believe that Genie actually got a story right."

Yikes. Never a good feeling to know there's another Hollywood Hype reader out there.

"For a change. Ha-ha."

He looks at me closely.

And knows I'm lying.

Greedy E hogged every ounce of acting talent in the family! Not even leaving me enough to put over a tiny white lie. Who cares if the Puppy Love story was as much a lie as any other?

I focus on rubbing Petunia's round belly. She rolls on her back, steps from heaven.

Jeremy still hasn't turned off his laser eyes. "No offense to Eva, but she's pretty . . . focused. Taking care of a pet for longer than a photo op? That's not on the agenda. So spill."

"It's no big deal. Eva had to go to Adopt-a-Stray for work." I tease Petunia with her toy, not looking at Jeremy. "That's where Petunia found me. Something about her—I knew she was for me."

I never contradict stories E has told the press, not to anyone—except for this once to Jeremy Jones because he mostly guessed anyway.

"It didn't cost me anything for Eva to say that Petunia was her dog."

I catch Jeremy's smile from the corner of my eye. "Now, *you* I can see with a dog." Jeremy's smile isn't as "famous" as my sister's, but it's still pretty nice.

He digs something out of his pocket. "I guess now I know who this was written for. One mystery solved."

Oh.

No.

OH FANFREAKING NO.

One of my poems. And he read it. One of my definitely-not-for-public-exposure poems.

"Um . . . that's not my paper."

"No? 'Cause it was on the ground near Eva's dressing room."
That proves nothing! Circumstantial evidence! Or possibly hear-
say! I'm still shaking my head when he adds, "Plus it has FROM THE
DESK OF JESSICA LUCIA ORTIZ printed across the top."

Worst.

Christmas present.

Ever.

Thanks a lot, Abuela.

I snatch back the poem and read it quickly. It's not as bad as
I feared.

It's worse. Earth-swallow-me-up-and-eat-me-now worse.

It is so clearly what it is: a love poem. To my dog.

Passing by the dog park,
Seeing proud Dalmatians,
Prancing poodles, not~so~Great Danes,
And the haughtiest Alsatians.

I look up and see the birds'
Joy in flight—sublime.

I'm reminded of you, new friend,
For the day's first time.

I can never look at Jeremy Jones again.

"C'mon, Jess, don't make that face."

"This *is* my face. I'm not making it."

I can never look at anyone who has ever looked at Jeremy Jones. I can never look at anyone who has ever looked at anyone who has looked at Jeremy Jones. (At this point, I kind of wish he hadn't been on international television for the past fifteen years in a row.)

"C'mon, don't be mad. Look, I'll write something. Then we're even, okay?"

I eye him suspiciously but hand him back the paper. Then I reach for my bag and pull out a pen.

I give him the pen. He thinks for a minute, tapping pen on paper and watching Petunia chase a bug, chunky legs pumping. Jeremy scribbles something and hands me back the paper.

Stubby-tailed doggie
Opposite of L.A.'s hype—
Happy and so fat.

Haiku?

I can't help it. I can't.

I burst out laughing.

"First off, Petunia is *big-boned*. And secondly, *haiku*?"

"Levi's commercial in Japan. Last Christmas break." Jeremy is smiling and shaking his head. "Jessica, I was so wrong about you. I can't believe I ever thought you . . ."

He doesn't finish the thought. He doesn't have to—he made it pretty clear what he suspected that day at the commissary.

"What? You can't believe you thought I'd sell incriminating pics of my own sister?"

He looks away, fast. But not fast enough.

Not before I read something in his eyes. Something bad.

Then he reaches into his pocket, self-consciously squeezing his cell phone.

I realize what he was thinking.

And it's so much worse than I thought.

Worse than I ever would have guessed if I hadn't seen the look on his face.

Jeremy—the person I trusted with the details of Project Stop Slander, whom *two minutes ago* I was spilling family secrets to—is someone very dangerous.

Dangerous to me.

I learn something. The hard way.

I learn that sometimes a clue isn't a fingerprint, or a locked door, or a new scent in the air. Sometimes a clue is about piecing together what someone thinks about the world, what he expects from other people, and putting it all together when a single flash of guilt moves over his face.

Jeremy didn't think I was just selling out my sister.

He thought I was *setting up* the stories, then selling them! He thought I was plowing down Hollywood's handsomest on purpose, snapping incriminating pictures of my own sister and selling the stories to the trashiest rag in town!

Okay, who suspects the Jones family may have some issues? Hands in the air, people.

Everything I know about Jeremy—and everything I'm beginning to guess—says he wouldn't stand by and let that happen. He'd keep his eyes open. He'd join me on a suspicious cart ride (Clooney). Bust in if I was talking to the crew (Kenny). Follow me (to the wardrobe, twice). Question me (commissary). And send me warnings:

```
I know what you're doing.
Stop now.

I'm watching you.
```

The text messages weren't sent to get me to quit Project Stop Slander. They were sent to get me to quit injuring people, and selling the stories.

Jeremy sees something of what I'm thinking on my face. He waits, alert as a hound.

The truth is sinking in, hard. "Jeremy, you sent me the text messages."

He doesn't try to play it off like a joke. A hot, red blush creeps up from his collar. "I'm sorry. I made a mistake. A bad one."

"You threatened me."

"I thought somebody was going to get seriously hurt, but I didn't have proof—"

"That's because there was no proof! Those were accidents!"

"I believe you, Jessica. I do. Now. You can't even guess how sorry I am."

"Jeremy, if you thought I was a danger to everyone on the show, and especially to my sister, why wouldn't you talk to Eva? Or my mom?"

A strange look moves across his eyes. Then his face is blank. Empty. "Your family would be the last people to believe me. Family always is."

He's right. My mom would have laughed him out of the room. She would have been right to do it, too.

Jeremy reaches for my arm. I jerk away as his fingers brush my skin. "Don't touch me. Don't talk to me."

I think about the two messages—one coming after the Clooney accident and article, the other after the *Angst* article. The Cal Anders accident should have triggered another warning—but it didn't. Jeremy and I had gone to lunch before that. He had started to believe that he had made a mistake about me.

Petunia thinks our fight is a kind of game, and she hops between us, looking for attention. I'm wondering what's going to happen next, when Paige and Lavender emerge from the limo.

"What's keeping Eva?" asks Paige. She is wearing a velvet V-neck top in lime green, beaded at the shoulders and center. Her black cropped pants look freshly pressed. As I look at her, my grass stains feel . . . grassier. "Hey, where'd that dog come from?"

Jeremy and I exchange looks. He says, "Eva adopted him at your Adopt-a-Stray event."

"Oh, that is *so* Brody," Paige says.

"Brody?"

"The OC's Adam Brody? He got his dog at an Adopt-a-Stray day. I mean, *I'm* not a trendmonger, but I can see how some people would copy him."

Lavender fusses with her purple hobo bag. She is dressed in a pantsuit that's the exact shade of a three-day-old bruise. Then she says, "Here comes Eva. Let's go, y'all."

Lavender, Paige, Eva, Jeremy Jones. And me.

A stretch limousine never felt so small.

Scene 6

Hollywood Boulevard, the world's most famous sidewalk. The Walk of Fame's star-studded sidewalks stretch for eighteen blocks along both sides of the boulevard, and along Vine Street, between Sunset Boulevard and Yucca Street. Each pink five-pointed star is embedded in a charcoal square. Right below the name of the celebrity on the star is a round category emblem: a motion picture camera, a television set, a record, a radio microphone, or the comedy-tragedy theater masks.

The *Two Sisters* photo shoot is being set up where the Walk of

Fame runs past Grauman's Chinese Theatre. The movie theater looks like a huge pagoda. Two massive orange columns hold up the bronze roof. Between the columns climbs a three-story dragon carved from stone. Guarding the theater entrance are two Chinese Heaven Dogs—and a shabby Spider-Man in frayed red rubber boots and a homemade blue and red costume.

Can you guess which of these doesn't belong?

The *Two Sisters* show runner can. Roman is supermad at the superhero.

The theater is a tourist spot, so it attracts out-of-work actors in costumes, rounding up tourists for uncomfortably posed ten-dollar Polaroids. Roman is negotiating to get Spider-Man out of the courtyard. The bargaining seems to consist of angry grimaces and a twenty-dollar bill.

The courtyard is a megapopular tourist destination because it is filled with the cement handprints and footprints of Hollywood legends—everyone from Marilyn Monroe to Donald Duck. (Webbed footprints in Donald's case.)

The lighting crew is setting up on the Walk of Fame, facing Grauman's. Kenny lugs equipment for Lighting Guy Bob, half-watching the pink stars under his feet. "Might be me someday. After film school." Does Spider-Man tell himself the same thing?

"Why not?" Lighting Guy Bob says with his usual scowl. "It happened to Big Bird. It could happen to you."

The area is finally secured and the actors are let out of the limo. (Seated next to Jeremy, I jumped out as soon as the limo slowed near the curb.) There is a flurry of camera flashes as the cast emerges. Security holds back the tourists, but the group signs autographs and poses for pictures before going into the trailers along the street for hair, makeup, and wardrobe.

I spot Keiko outside a trailer, banging away on her BlackBerry.

"Hi, Keiko."

She glances up. Nods.

"Sorry again about that tea spill."

She nods again, keeps punching buttons.

"Keiko, can I ask you a question?"

Nod.

There is something on my mind: she knew my cell number, and she gave me that "secret admirer" nudge-nudge-wink.

"Did Jeremy Jones ask you for my phone number?"

Nod. Followed by a quick look. "Anything you want to publicize? I mean, it's obvious what he thinks, but you've been harder to read."

"No. Nothing to . . . publicize. We're just"—*enemies forever!*—"friends."

"Okay, 'cause there could be a story there. Sister-of-the-star stuff." Keiko pays me a morsel more attention. " 'Cause you . . . what? Sing? Dance? Weave?"

"No, I go to school. Holy Sisters Academy in the fall."

"Oh." Keiko spots my mom arriving at the theater. "Your mom and I are meeting with the photographer to go over layouts. Stay out of trouble."

Keiko gets pretty plainspoken when Eva isn't around. And what happened to all the exclamation points? As Genie would say, still tea-ed off?

Speaking of plain speaking, I turn around to see Roman's face plainly telling me that he doesn't want me here. His face is especially easy to read because it's about two inches from my own. Our noses are almost touching.

A blue pulse is beating at the edge of his eye as he tries to think of the exact horrible words to say to me.

My mind just blanks.

That's why I say what I say.

Even though I shouldn't.

Pointing over his shoulder, I say, "Isn't that Wonder Woman?"

Then I bolt for the nearest souvenir shop. Not my bravest moment, but not my dumbest either. I keep one eye out the window of the shop to make sure Lavender doesn't get by me. I'm looking through "Best Dad" Oscar statues and overpriced magnets when I hear his voice.

Not Roman's voice, but one I should run away from all the same.

"Jessica, can we talk?"

I turn. "Jeremy? Aren't you supposed to be getting ready?"

He looks down at his jeans and T-shirt. "I am ready."

Sometimes guys get the easier gig.

Every tourist in the souvenir shop gets quiet. I can practically see one old lady's ears twitching up under her wig.

"Okay."

We head back into the courtyard. Just for something to do, we find ourselves crouching over Julie Andrews's cement prints, following her twirling signature with our fingers.

"Jess, I'm so sorry. It was some kind of mistaken identity thing." Jeremy keeps his eyes on the ground. "You probably can't relate."

Can you say "Keiko"?

"I can relate. A little."

"Yeah?" His face brightens. He looks less like a brooding TV teen and more like a real person.

"About Eva? You know those dating rumors were never true, right?"

"The journalists at *Twist* somehow got it all wrong, huh?"

Jeremy grins. "Eva is great—seriously—but do you ever think she's really . . . driven?"

"Nope." Like I'm going to admit anything more about my family to him!

"Oh," says Jeremy. "Well, it's just an impression I had. Anyway, let's not talk about Eva."

I don't see how we can avoid Eva, since she is the only thing we have in common. Besides that we both have protective streaks, we're naturally inquisitive, love dogs, sometimes make enormous mistakes about people, and laugh a lot if we're not driving each other crazy.

Before I can say another word, I notice that Jeremy's fingers are brushing against mine, right where the *w* curves into the *s*. And his face is suddenly close. He's blocking my view of the street.

"Um . . . Jeremy?"

"Jessica," he says softly, and he's still coming closer, until I can feel his breath on my cheek, and his fingers sliding into mine, and now—

"*Hello, Jeremy and Eva!*" howls a voice, drawing the attention of every tourist, crew member, and low-flying airplane. With zero subtlety, Lavender snaps a picture with her cell phone.

Jeremy pulls away from me. Quick.

Suddenly my quarry is stalking me. Lavender taps closer on her high heels. She peers at me in faux surprise over the top of her bulky plum sunglasses.

"Oh, it's you," drawls Lavender. "You can see why Ah naturally *assumed* you were Eva. Oh, this is so *awkward*." She savors the word *awkward* like the last bonbon in the box. "Don't worry, y'all. This will be our little secret."

"There is no 'this,' " Jeremy says, but Lavender is already tramping away. He turns to me. "Forget her, Jess. She's just annoying."

"No, she isn't. She's a threat to my sister." I wasn't quick enough to get mad at Lavender, so it's all coming out at Jeremy. "I was supposed to be catching her, not the other way around!"

Then can you guess who jumps from a trailer to the courtyard in Jeremy's defense?

No, it's not Spider-Man—though I spot him and his Polaroid camera sneaking away from the scene.

"Leave him alone, Jessica." Paige's green eyes are snapping. "We're like an orchestra here and no one instrument can play on its own."

Well, that shuts Jeremy and me up for a moment.

Then Paige dips her head toward Jeremy, waggling her sunflower earrings. "As for you, Jeremy Jones, the answer is . . . maybe."

What was the question?

Jeremy looks as if he doesn't know the question either. He does know that he doesn't want to stick around and be yelled at. Even when he deserves it.

He heads over to hide out with—I mean, *consult with*—Lighting Guy Bob and the crew. The actresses bond with the stylists, and the actors with the technical and construction crew.

After a while, Eva emerges from the trailer, pressed, primped, perfect. The cast poses with the Chinese lions, in the ornate doorway, and even at the souvenir shop. There are snaps of them lying on the Walk of Fame sidewalk—taken after much mopping by the crew. The photo shoot runs long, and Lighting Guy Bob makes sour jokes about needing an infrared camera to see in the dark.

But all through the long afternoon and into the evening, there is only one photo on my mind. The one that will be appearing in Hollywood Hype in the morning. Will it be as bad as I think?

Or worse?

"Good morning, Jessica."

I feel like telling Mali there is not much chance of that. While she is feeding wheatgrass into the juicer, I head to the *Los Angeles Record,* primly folded on the breakfast table.

I open to Hollywood Hype just as Mali hits Grind on the juicer.

Goofy expression.

Eyes half closed.

Something smudged on my cheek.

Wind-messed hair.

Not my best photo, so of course it's the first one ever printed in a newspaper. In this terrible photo, Jeremy and I look closerthanthis, and Genie Wolff's headline screams:

Sister to Sister

Eva Ortiz's long-rumored boyfriend, Jeremy Jones, was caught canoodling with

> the Latin lovely's own
> sister at a Hollywood photo
> shoot yesterday. Hype says,
> "Two sisters? Too much!"

How am I going to face Eva? I've become the bad press I'm trying to protect her from. I want to hide under my bed until it's a better day, but I don't want Eva to see the column before I can talk to her.

I hear the outdoor shower and guess that Eva has gone for a morning run. Running puts her in a good mood, so she is whistling to herself when she comes into the kitchen, wrapped in a towel.

I watch her for a moment, letting her enjoy these last few moments of happiness before the remorseless hammer of—

"Hey, didja see Hollywood Hype this morning?" she asks me. "Not your best picture, Jess."

I respond thoughtfully. "Hummanahummanhumma . . ."

"So I called Keiko first thing," Eva continues. "I told her to release the story that I was never dating Jeremy—just trying to set him up with my sister. She thinks *Teen People* might want to pick it up, y'know, as a 'good sister' kind of story."

I guess I shouldn't be surprised that my sister can take lemons and turn them into a multimillion-dollar self-promotion campaign.

Eva is warming to her theme. "I told them about how I saw that you two would be a great couple, since you both love animals, have that same weird sense of humor, and—"

"E!" I have to interrupt her. "Jeremy and I had a huge fight yesterday and are never, ever speaking to each other again!"

At that moment, Mom enters. "Phone for you, Jess. It's Jeremy Jones."

Eva arches one perfectly plucked eyebrow at me.

I grab the phone. Before I can say anything more than hello, I hear Jeremy's voice. "It's not Lavender."

"Yes, I know it's not Lavender. It's Jeremy, right?"

Jeremy is talking fast. "When I saw that photo, I knew Lavender couldn't have taken it. She was standing right in front of us, and the photo was taken from an angle and farther back."

"Are you sure?"

"Of course I'm sure. That photo is from the moment we were about to kiss. She couldn't be the leaker. At least not on this story."

I don't know what to say.

"Jessica? Are you there?"

I don't know what to say.

"Hello? Jess?"

Jeremy Jones had been about to kiss me!

"Um . . . hello?" Jeremy gives up and the phone clicks off in my hand. Eva is still looking at me. "E," I whisper, "Jeremy Jones likes me."

"Hello, Captain Oblivious," Eva says. "I saw that coming a mile away."

"Two miles for me," adds Mom, who reenters stage left carrying the fake books from the library in a big donation box.

She puts down the box to give me a hug. "Jessica, maybe this is a sign that you should pay more attention to your own life. You might be missing out on some lovely things."

"Mom, you're right." I haven't been seeing things clearly, but that's going to change, starting now. "It's time to wrap up Project Stop Slander—for Eva, for Jeremy, and for *me*."

I'm already heading up the stairs to start my plan.

"Um . . . Mom, is this progress?" asks Eva.

"I'm not sure," says Mom.

But I am.

Act
V

If you ask people what they've always wanted to do,
most people haven't done it. That breaks my heart.

—ANGELINA JOLIE

M otive. Means. Opportunity.
Every criminal has them.

I go over the clues I have, watching for those three pieces to come into play.

Money, revenge, or both could have motivated the leaks to Hollywood Hype and the stolen gown. The culprit would need regular access to the *Two Sisters* set.

The dress thief and the slanderer might be the same person, or not. There might even be more than one slanderer—Lavender could have sold the earlier stories even if she didn't sell the last one.

I go over the physical evidence: the lock on the wardrobe set to Paige's birthday; the bead from the gown hidden in the wardrobe; the scent of fresh flowers; Eva's "lost" audition DVD.

I go over my questioning of cast and crew. Alibis. Excuses.

And then . . . I remember a moment in the investigation that ties into another moment right here at home. That gets me thinking.

But how can I be sure?

I'm wondering which move to make next when inspiration comes from an unexpected source.

The U.S. mail.

The package is small, brown, and square. From the way Petunia sniffs it and walks away, there is zero possibility that it is food-related.

It's the first piece of personal mail that has been sent to me at my new address. I run up to my room to open it in private.

When I tear into it, a thin, photocopied booklet falls onto my bed, along with a letter. Familiar scratchy handwriting scrawls across a torn-out sheet of lined notebook paper.

Jess,
  I SUCK At GOODBYes. You
noticeD?
  Sorry I DiDN't ResponD to YOUR
e-mails/texts. I Know that must
Be pulling YOUR wig. It WOULD hAve

Been hard to pretend you're off
on vacation if you're on the
other end of the line telling me
about your plush new
B.H. life.
   I don't know how to start
back—can't roll into your
kitchen and start raiding
the fridge. But you're the
first person I wanted to show
this to.
   Don't let the Hollywood heads
get to you.

                              —Leo

With the letter is a photocopy of Leo's zine. Leo would define
a zine as an economically produced, self-published (read:
Kinko's) underground publication. His version looks like a mini
graphic novel with black-and-white illustrations, photocopied,
folded, and stapled together.

All along I had thought the title was *Anaheim Avenger*.

So I'm surprised the big square letters on the front cover spell out *Avenger and Poet*.

When he was working on it, I would throw out ideas for the female character. Leo was pretty secretive, but I figured she was a quiet sidekick. Barely even a Robin to Avenger's Batman. (I should say Rogue to his Wolverine; Leo would prefer it.) But in the finished zine, she's a real partner. She's even the one who first cracks Blackslash's evil caper. Poet suspects that the hot tip about the stolen plutonium can't be trusted; that it's all a trap. Avenger doesn't listen. He goes off on his own and winds up trapped in Blackslash's underground lair. Will Poet come back to rescue him?

And that's how the story ends. With a dramatic "To be continued . . ."

I have to admit I'm pleased that Poet is stronger and smarter than I had expected. And Leo has done a great job with the illustration; the lines are polished—angular and tight—contrasted with rough-edged hand-lettering for the type.

I'm reaching for my phone to give Leo a call when I take a closer look at how Poet is drawn. She's pretty much a babe. Which makes me happy—until I realize that she's got Eva's (old) superlong hair, and her rounder eyes. And the way she's standing on page two, panel four, hands on hips, head cocked, is pure E!

I click the phone off.

I can really miss Leo and still want to sock him a Poet punch, can't I?

*A*venger and *Poet* shows me the way.

I can't sit around waiting for the next lie to hit the press or theft to hit the set. It's time for action.

It's time for a trap.

If my guess about the culprit is right, the big Banks party tonight will be the perfect time to strike, and I should be able to dangle the right bait.

But I can't do it on my own.

I know who I have to call. He picks up on the second ring.

"Hello, Watson. It's Holmes here."

"Katie!" Jeremy says. "Hi! I'm a *huge* fan—"

"Jeremy, it's *Jessica*. I was making a literary reference. Informed people know who Sherlock Holmes and Whatshisname Watson are."

Pause.

"Hi, Jessica." His voice is guarded. Miles less enthusiastic. "What's up?"

"I need your help." I know what you're thinking, but this was not an excuse to call him. When I thought about it, Jeremy was the best one to help.

I tell Jeremy my plan.

He doesn't laugh me off the line, but he's not convinced either.

"It's the best idea you've had so far." Happiness starts to bubble, until he adds, "That doesn't mean it's a good idea. You'll have to do some running around on the set to pull this off."

"That's no problem," I say confidently. After a moment, I add, "Any special guest stars this week?"

"Ashley and Mary-Kate Olsen."

We are both quiet for a moment while we consider the petite fragility of the Olsen twins' sister-empire.

"No worries." I hope I sound convincing.

"Probably nothing to be concerned about," Jeremy agrees. "And besides, they must be sturdier than they look."

Worst.

Pep talk.

Ever.

"Jessica, I'll help you because your trap could work. But I think you're wrong about who you'll catch."

I think I'm right. And I'm willing to bet on it.

Is Jeremy?

*F*or some reason it feels right to make the next call from the formal dining room. We never eat there. The room has two large square wood tables surrounded by armless plush chairs, set under a crystal-and-iron chandelier, surrounded by museum-ish wall hangings. A bit much for our usual tacos and guac. But not for what I'm trying to pull off.

"Bonjour?" Hélène answers.

I let her know what I want: for her to get the word out about an expensive piece of jewelry that will accompany Eva's lavender jersey gown.

She turns me down flat. The whole idea offends, appalls, and dismays.

"The cut of the dress is so simple, Jessica. A flashy piece will overwhelm the look entirely! The eye will not know where to look, what to appreciate! Don't you understand what it means when 'Costume Supervisor: Hélène Marcy' flashes in the credits?"

Once I explain that I'm not talking about accessories, I'm talking about bait, Hélène is on board faster than you can say Coco Chanel.

"A diamond tiara from Harry Winston!" she exclaims. "I'll start spreading the word that I'm renting one. Of course, anyone with fashion sense would realize that a tiara spells disaster for Eva's ensemble, but I don't think we have to worry about that kind of insight in this case. *Oui?*"

Oui.

*A*nd speaking of limited fashion sense . . .
"Dad?"

I've tracked my dad down in his lair: the workbench at the back of the garage. Something about being outnumbered three females to one male sends Dad down here at least twice a day.

With Eva's posh party tonight, Dad took this afternoon off.

"Hi, Jessica." He's running sandpaper over raw wood and gets a hopeful look on his face when I appear. "Did you want to help with the birdhouse?"

"No, Dad. I'm sure it will be great." I am sure. Dad built Eva and me a playhouse that was better constructed than our real house; when we go to the beach, his sand castles are such masterworks of engineering that other families come by to get their picture taken in front of them. As Leo would say, the man's got mad skillz.

And I've got a use for them.

"Dad, I think I know who has been selling those stories about Eva."

"Good news. What did your mom say?"

"I haven't told Mom yet." That gets his attention. "I need proof. And I could use your help to get it."

"Me?"

So I tell him my plan, carefully explaining his part. How the wardrobe is deep and made of dark oak.

He wants to tell Mom.

"Dad, she'd want to take care of it her way—the drive-through-the-front-door, get-everybody-involved way." I look him in the eye. "But we need proof. We've got to be thorough. That's what *we're* good at, right?"

He nods. He knows he's being played to, but he doesn't seem to mind.

He has a few Dad-like conditions:

I carry a press-button siren so that I can sound an alarm if needed.

He has to be nearby when it all goes down.

We double-check the infrared recording function on the family video camera.

And, no matter if the trap succeeds or fails, I personally have to apologize to Roman about any malfunction with the Megatron television. (Rhyme optional.)

We go over every part of the plan. Twice.

With Dad on board, it's time for the most painful part of the assignment to begin.

"**O**www!"

I was attached to those eyebrows. Literally.

Getting gorgeous is not for the faint of heart.

Even if you're Eva and start out with a solid base of natural beauty, there are still makeup, hair, prodding, primping, pulling, and pain that have to go on. Styling duo Mary and Steve have made an in-home visit to wrangle Eva into starworthy shape, and Eva asked them to "help" my look as well.

That's why Steve and his iron have ensured that I now have swirling smooth locks that whisper against my face. I could re-create this look myself at any time—any time I have eight arms and eyes behind my head, that is.

Uh-oh, now Mary is moving in with her colorful palette.

"Um, E, I think I'll do my own makeup," I whisper.

"A swipe of cherry lip gloss isn't going to do it tonight, Jess." Out of Mary's hearing she adds, "Don't worry, she has to layer on the makeup on the set for the cameras. She'll go lighter on you."

Mary chats away as she applies her colors and brushes: a shimmery violet eye shadow, black kohl eyeliner—thin—and an almost-plum lipstick. Then a rose-colored blush and bronzing powder all over. Maybe the finished result looks light to Eva, but I'm not used to so much color on my face. In the mirror, my eyes look huge and surprised.

I'd say that I was sweating out the process, except I can't sweat because Hélène surprised me with my first-ever, tailored-for-me glamour gown. Hélène described it as "floating tiers of fuchsia chiffon." The rich, hot pink falls in soft layers to midcalf, more fitted on top, with superskinny straps. The silver high-heeled sandals are hard to walk in but very sparkly. Around my wrist is a charm bracelet. (I saved $990 getting it from Claire's Accessories instead of Fred Segal.)

Once my face is camera-ready, we head to Eva's room, and I help her into her dress, a slim-fitting light blue knee-length sheath with spaghetti straps. Mom is big on straps—it doesn't matter how skinny they are, they've just got to be there.

Eva looks at our reflections in the mirror. "That dress is spectacular. How did you get so popular with Hélène?"

By going after the dress thief. "Hélène? She likes me, I guess."

I don't say another word.

Jeremy, Hélène, Dad, and one other person know about my plans tonight. Eva is not the one other person.

scene 4

The back of the studio-audience theater is set up for the party. Forget Craft Services and Krispy Kremes. Tonight there are butlered hors d'oeuvres of lollipop lamb chops, seared ahi

214

tuna on crackers, and wild mushroom tartlets. There is even a caviar and vodka bar. (It turns out the Banks family is Russian. When Grandpa Banks got off the boat, he decided to take the name of the fanciest building he saw: the bank. They never looked back.)

Mom looks pretty in her simple black dress. She is making uneasy small talk with Paula and Keiko. Dad told her he was going to park the car; he didn't mention the extra errand he's going on.

"Doesn't look good," Eva whispers to me.

For a minute, I think she's referring to Lavender's gray-purple strapless gown—supertight on top, flared at the hips, and falling to the knee in shaggy triangles of fabric.

"Yikes. What color is that? Grapple?"

"Just keep an eye on her." Eva's eyes scan me again. "Jessica, does your dress have something to do with tonight's plan?"

How does she know? How does she *always* know? "Plan?"

"To get the audition DVD back. If Lavender has been selling me out to Genie, she isn't going to be above playing that DVD at the party."

"Dad is on it."

"Dad!"

"Yep, he's going to disable the Megatron screen."

"Did you tell him *why*?" Eva is freaking.

"He has no idea about the audition. Don't worry."

"Dad is going to *break* something?"

"Temporarily disable. With a remote control."

"Doesn't that go against his mechanic's oath?" She gives me a long look. "What did you tell him?"

"I told him that"—I check my watch—"we're running out of time."

Eva looks around. "Where is he? Are you telling me everything?"

"Yes." Mostly.

I didn't want Eva to even know there was a Project Stop Slander until I had actually *stopped slander*. I wasn't able to keep that secret, and multiple disasters followed. Tonight I have a fresh chance. I can surprise some of the people I'd like to impress: Eva. Mom. Keiko the Capable. The crew.

If everything goes right.

Eva isn't going to let this lie. "Listen, Jessica—"

"Listen to what?" Jeremy appears, wearing a midnight blue button-down shirt with French cuffs over black pants.

"Hi, Jeremy."

Eva presses her lips together. "I'm going to talk to Keiko. She always knows what's going on."

When Eva stomps off, I tell Jeremy, "Thanks for your help with the plan. For a guy who looks like Jolly Old Saint Nick—"

"—he can act like a real Grinch."

Jeremy had texted me a brief message: "The lights are ON."

We both smile, and Jeremy is about to say something more when his pant leg gets a tug from the bottom.

You'd recognize Jeremy's six-year-old brother if you saw him: chubby cheeks; enormous brown eyes; spiky white-blond hair. You've seen him in TV movies and commercials. In the TV movies, his mom/dog/goldfish dies; in the commercials, everyone survives.

Jeremy crouches to look his brother in the eye. Improbably, Jack squats down as well.

"Hey, buddy, having fun?" Jeremy asks.

Jack Jones pulls his chubby fists from his pockets. They are stuffed with sugar packets in various colors. "I got pink, blue, white, and purple." I guess there's not much else for him to do here.

I get a sudden glimpse into Jeremy's life. He's been working since he was *this small*. Even this party is a job.

"Look at this, Jack." Jeremy pulls out a brown sugar packet. "One more for you." I can guess who taught Jack all about packet collecting. "Say hello to Jessica."

Jack stands and solemnly extends his little hand. "Pleased to meet you."

"And you," I say formally. I lean closer to him and breathe in peanut butter and some undefined, uniquely small-boy smell. No one in the room smells like him.

"Mom wants me," Jack says.

Following his look, I see a tall, tight-faced blonde with a shiny smile. She is cueing Jack with hand signals like an animal trainer while holding Roman by the wrist.

If this is a window into Jeremy's life, somebody draw the curtains. Jack heads back to his mom, disappearing quickly among the pant legs and dress bottoms.

I look at Jeremy. There's pretty much only one thing you can say after meeting Jack Jones. "Wow, he's cuter than a box of puppies."

Jeremy gives a self-mocking grin. "Don't let my mom hear you say that. She'll have Jack passing out business cards with that slogan."

"Really?" I look at him curiously.

Jeremy nods. "Keeping up with the Joneses takes on a new meaning with my mom."

Instinctively I know he wants to move the subject away from his family. So I say, "Showtime."

The guests of honor have arrived: Mr. Banks—ancient, white-haired, wealthy; and Mrs. Banks—not so much.

The groom smiles at his young bride, and raises a champagne flute in the direction of our show runner. "Thanks for throwing this party together, Roman. When Lola said *Two Sisters* was her favorite show, I couldn't think of a better way to surprise her on her birthday . . ."

Polite clapping.

". . . than by giving her full control of the show!"

Horrified silence.

"Just kidding!"

Polite laughter, muffling the sound of Roman's heart restarting.

Hélène takes this as her cue to cut through the crowd. She is wearing a floor-length blue Cinderella gown with sheer bell sleeves and holding a Harry Winston box. "Mrs. Banks, I heard that you are starting a jewelry collection and couldn't resist showing you this beautiful piece."

Hélène opens the velvet box and lifts out a sparkling diamond tiara. Gently, she places it atop Mrs. Banks's head.

"Fit for a queen," Hélène trills.

"Fit for a vault!" Mr. Banks says, getting a laugh. But his eyes are serious as he removes the jewelry.

The tiara is put back into the box. Hélène murmurs a polite "Adieu" and disappears backstage.

Roman taps his champagne flute to get everyone's attention. "Now we're going to watch an exclusive clip from our upcoming season."

Eva flashes me a nervous look, but Dad is back in the room. He pats the remote scrambler in his pocket. If Lavender has done anything strange to the reel (i.e., swapped it out for Eva's secret audition DVD), he can scramble the TV before anyone knows what they're looking at.

Why would Dad do that?

Because I told him there was a chance that the leaker might try to slip in some kind of fake, E-incriminating scene—to make some news to sell to Genie. This was basically a lie, but my dad never doubted me. Maybe acting is in my blood. But if it always gives you that guilty, gut-clenching feeling, it's not for me.

The crowd starts to gather around the Megatron. That's my cue.

I slip the pocket alarm on its string out of my clutch and around my neck. I make my way toward the stage. I'm being discreet until—

"That's so J.Lo."

"Hi, Paige."

"That charm bracelet? A total knockoff of the one Jennifer Lopez wears. Except hers is Louis Vuitton."

Paige's blond locks are teased into an enormous halo. Her psychedelic bell-bottomed pantsuit is matched with demure pearls and pumps. (I had sensed fashion danger for Paige when this month's *Vogue* declared both the Jackson Five and Jackie Kennedy back in style.)

"*You* are calling *me* a trend slave?"

"If the bracelet fits." Paige has got me cornered and is warming up for a fashion lecture.

I'm stuck.

"What's around your neck? A Kabbalah string?"

I'm *so* stuck.

Enter Jeremy. "Hey, Paige, did you hear that Versace is going to start making clothes for Wal-Mart?"

Paige whirls on him, confusion in her eyes. "What?"

I step back, smoothly, stealthily, farther, farther . . .

Jeremy throws an arm around Paige's shoulder and turns her away from me. A small pillbox hat clings to the back of her kinked hair.

He starts improvising. "I read it online this morning. Donatella thinks all the skirt and shorts lines should be merged into skorts. That would save time for the busy Wal-Mart shopper. . . ."

I make a break for backstage. I've snuck into one of the quiet corridors when suddenly I see the two people who could ruin everything.

The two people who must not see me.

The two people who are a danger to my plan—and to themselves.

It's Dualstar empire-actresses Mary-Kate and Ashley Olsen.

Whoa.

There aren't many people who make me feel tall, but looming over them, I feel large, and worse—threatening.

"Hello," Mary-Kate says. Or is it the other one? "We're looking for the Banks party?"

Agitated, I back up against the wall. "Please, don't come near me," I whisper.

"Would you know where . . . ? What did you say?"

"Please," I hiss. "In the name of all that is *Full House*, stay away from me, or disaster will strike!" I look around for signs of imminent crisis.

"Um . . . okay." Now they are both slowly backing away. "Take it

222

easy." They're quite nice about the whole thing—though I do think I hear one mutter something about "Red Bull overload."

I creep back toward my position. There is the wardrobe. Checking over my shoulder—no one around—I slip inside. Dad hid our family's video camera under a couple of stuffed emus. I pick up the camera and examine the other new addition to the wardrobe: a false back.

Dad cut a thin board to fit inside the wardrobe. The board has a small square cut out of it. I wedge myself behind the board and place the eye of the video camera in the square.

And then I wait.

A few minutes later, I hear, "Back to the party for me!"

Hélène doesn't usually talk to herself, or even walk past this part of the corridor—but she can't resist sending me a signal.

And then I wait. And wait some more.

I'm not sure of the time, but it seems as though the Megatron screening must be rolling right along. During the show, when all eyes are on the screen, that's when I expect . . . *step-step step-step step-step* . . . to hear footsteps.

Coming right toward me.

he wardrobe creaks open. In the darkness, he doesn't seem to notice that the space is about a foot less deep than it was before. That the back of the wardrobe isn't perfectly aligned with the walls.

I peer through the camera's viewfinder. In the infrared light, I can see what he's carefully placing at the bottom of the wardrobe. A Harry Winston box.

He is looking over his shoulder. His muscles are tensed as if he can feel someone watching, as if he knows something is not right, but what?

Then he pulls out something I wasn't prepared for.

A small flashlight hooked onto a thick ring of keys.

I watch the round beam scan the back of the wardrobe, and I almost think I'm going to make it. I almost think I'm going to be okay.

Then my viewfinder fills with light, and I know he's seeing the light bounce off the glass eye of my camera.

His hand, shaking, reaches toward the camera. The camera's picture is filling with thick, approaching fingers.

So I do the only thing I can do.

I fall forward.

I go crashing through the false back of the wardrobe. My hip bangs on the Harry Winston box, and I hear a definite *crunch*. The camera drops away as I roll practically into the thief's lap. He's sprawled under the board, and under me.

It must be for only the smallest slice of second that our eyes meet, but his surprise and anger chill me.

"You!" He slides out from under the board and reaches for my shoulders. I can feel his fingers digging, yanking me to my feet. Now his hands are creeping north, toward my neck.

Where is that alarm? I squeeze a hand between our bodies and grasp the string holding the alarm. Then I find the button and

WAAAAAAAAAAAAAAAAAAAAAAAAA!

A piercing wail rings through the corridor.

Dad and Hélène arrive in an instant. They were waiting just on the other side of the outside door, the one Jeremy pulled me through when we went to lunch.

My dad grabs my assailant, knocks him onto his back, and has him tied up in coarse rope in about twenty seconds. That knot will hold. It looks like the one Dad used on my Anaheim tree swing.

Hélène cries, "Jessica, you did it! You caught . . ."

She gets a good look at the thief's face.

"Kenny?"

The lighting technician. I guess I should have expected the flashlight.

"You can't prove anything!" Kenny yells.

"Kenny, we have you on video, putting the tiara into the wardrobe. And then you attacked me!"

"I was helping you up after you fell."

"By the neck?"

Dad is starting to growl.

"Besides, someone is coming who you're going to *want* to explain things to."

I think there is a person who can make Kenny confess the truth and save the police some time. Especially if he doesn't notice that I never turned off the video camera.

I take out my cell and call Jeremy.

He must run down the hall, because both he and the person he's bringing are out of breath when they appear.

"Whew!" Paige says, rounding the corner. "I mean I like an eager date and all, but . . ."

She looks around the corridor. "What's everybody doing back here? Did something else get stolen?"

"Yes," I say. "By Kenny."

"Kenny?"

The hard look on Kenny's face falls away. "Paige, please, I can explain."

"You can?"

"I'm going to film school in the fall, but why should we have to wait till I'm a famous director to be together?"

Um . . . 'cause then Paige might remember who you are.

I can see Paige isn't tracking. "Paige, *Kenny* is your secret admirer."

"Kenny? But I thought . . ." Her eyes flicker to Jeremy. For a moment, she doesn't look like Paige Carey, ever-gorgeous model-actress. She looks surprised, bewildered, disappointed. The expression on her face reminds me of: me. "Kenny, what were you thinking?"

He gulps. "Does this mean we're not on for the Hollywood Bowl?"

I jump in. "Paige, it's worse than you think. Kenny was stealing from the set to buy you presents—Hélène's gown, the tiara. And he was selling stories to Hollywood Hype."

Paige's nose wrinkles. Kenny looks at her with his heart in his eyes. Believing his fate rests less on a police investigation than on her next few words.

Paige frowns. "That's *so* direct-to-video."

Ouch!

Kenny hangs his head. He thinks the moment can't get any worse.

He's wrong.

"So it was true!"

Lighting Guy Bob is hustling down the corridor as fast as his belly will allow.

He lets out a snarl, moving toward Kenny, but Hélène gets there first. "Where is my dress? Where is it?"

Caught between a French costumer and her couture clothing?

Kenny will be begging the police to take him away.

*M*om, Dad, Eva, and Keiko: the expressions on their faces are everything I could have hoped for. Curious, pleased, and impressed.

Along with Paige and Jeremy, we're squeezed around one of the dining tables at the back of the theater. "So how did you figure it out?" Eva asks.

"Actually, Jeremy provided me with my first clue."

"I did?" Jeremy looks surprised.

"Yes, it was when I was asking people where they had been when the gown was stolen."

I take them through my trail of clues. First, when I asked Kenny where he'd been during the theft, he said he had been working on the large white spotlight all morning. But when Jeremy leaned on the light, it wasn't hot. He rested his hand right on it. This didn't register with me till later when Mom felt my hot television and busted me for clocking excessive TV time.

I put that puzzle together with the physical evidence. The bead told me that the stolen gown had been stashed in the wardrobe.

The scent of flowers in the wardrobe, along with the lock that was set to Paige's birthday, told me that her secret-admirer gifts spent some time there, too. So it was possible that the secret admirer and the thief were the same person. If they were the same person, the thief might be motivated by cash to get Paige more pricey presents.

There were a few other pieces that pointed to Kenny. He's a short guy, and the key was hidden at my eye level. One of the notes mentions a big life change. I thought that might be something else. (I flash a guilty look at Jeremy and his haircut.) But it could have been Kenny's move to film school. Plus he delivered a gift to Paige at Adopt-a-Stray.

It seemed crazy that someone would take all those chances—cross all those lines—for someone who barely registers them. But then I thought of some fan sites I'd seen. Sometimes people think they really know a celebrity, as if the person is their best friend or potential prom date or something. And Kenny was closer than an average fan: He worked on set. He saw Paige in person every day, even if she never saw him.

But I wanted to be sure.

I asked Dad to help me hide in the wardrobe with the video camera. I asked Jeremy for help with Lighting Guy Bob. Bob was the fourth and final person in on the plan. I wouldn't have had much chance convincing Bob of anything, but Jeremy gets along well with the crew. I needed Bob to make sure Kenny wasn't too busy. That he could have time and access to the backstage area—if he wanted them.

After I'm done with my explanation, everybody takes a deep breath.

Eva reaches over to squeeze my shoulders tight. "You really came through, Jess," she says in a proud, low voice.

I put on my best Hollywood accent and whisper back, "Hey, babe, who's your sister?"

Mom turns to Dad. She's not whispering. "And you knew all about this, Robert?"

Neither Dad nor I can tell if she's mad. Or if she's not mad now but will get mad if she thinks about it.

"You know the old expression, Susan. 'Keep your friends close and your daughters closer.' "

I thought it was keep your *enemies* closer?

At any rate, Mom and Dad exchange a look, and then Mom decides to laugh. *Whew!*

Keiko pops a piece of California roll into her mouth. "You're incredible, babe. But you really took a risk with that tiara."

"For forty bucks it was worth it."

Lots of widened eyes.

"Claire's Accessories makes one fine diamondesque tiara," I explain.

"Ha!" Mom laughs. "We should tell Mrs. Banks that. She didn't look too happy to have to give it up."

Everybody is toasting me and cheering. When suddenly the moment turns . . . lavender.

Lavender Wells appears.

"Have a minute, Eva?"

Eva is out of her chair in an instant, hustling Lavender away from our parents. I'm right behind her.

"Good news, Eva. Look what Ah found." Lavender reaches into her bag and pulls out a DVD. The audition DVD.

Eva tries to stay cool but can't help snapping it out of Lavender's fingers. "Where was it?"

"It had slipped into a side compartment of mah bag. Ah took a look at your work, sugar. Very inspiring. Too bad—"

Eva's eyes are alert. "Too bad what?"

"You didn't hear?"

Eva shakes her head.

"Scarlett Johansson got the part."

"Oh." Eva gets smaller right in front of my eyes. Despite everything—Mom and Dad forbidding her to take the part, the stolen audition DVD, the A-list competition—Eva believed that she and *Wisconsin Girl* were meant to be together. "Scarlett's so—"

"Overrated," Eva and Lavender say at the same time, with matching half smiles. *Overrated* is jealous-actress-speak for *talented*.

Envy is usually a force for pushing actresses apart; for the first time I see it bringing Eva and Lavender together, uniting them in jealousy of a bigger star.

"That script was entirely lame."

"The lead character was flatter than a dirt road."

"And twice as boring."

"You can type that junk, but you can't say it."

"What was with that dialogue?"

"You're right, shug."

"You too, Lavender. See you on the set?"

"Of course. Nice dress. The Green Diet is so working for you."

"Thanks. Mischa Barton didn't look as good in those shoes."

The odd thing is, as jealous as the *Two Sisters* team can get of one another, the show is working because of some indefinable chemistry between them. No one could pinpoint why it works. Kind of like real sisters.

And so . . . no catfight in the pool or kung fu kick-out—not even a simple "Oh, it's on, boo!" Despite all the envy, competing, and cheating, tomorrow Eva and Lavender will be back to *Two Sisters,* ready to play their roles.

As for how I feel about Lavender . . . *oh, it's on, boo!*

Lavender and Eva glide off to get a drink. I'm about to tag along when a grip hands me a cranberry soda.

Someone on the set likes me! Someone to speak up for me! Someone to give me the benefit of the doubt! Someone to . . . run away when he sees Roman bearing down on me, eyes flashing.

"Miss Ortiz, what was it about hosting our financier tonight that made you think it was the perfect opportunity for your little caper?"

Shy spasm hits.

But I fight through it, squeezing out a few words: "Well, Kenny knew everyone would be distracted, and it was a good chance to get the tiara out. . . ."

Roman gives me a withering gaze, breathing hard in my face. "That was a rhetorical question, babe," he bites out.

The kind you don't want an answer to. Got it.

Someday I'll be able to tell *shy spasm* apart from *common sense*.

Yeesh. I flop down onto the seat next to Keiko. Our table has cleared out—everyone heading toward the temporary dance floor they've put on the stage.

"Good work tonight, babe!" she says. She reaches into her bag and pulls out a pink envelope. "This is for you."

A card? Did the *Two Sisters* group sign a *card* for me? Even for Keiko the Capable, that was fast. And really, I was just happy to contribute, and wasn't expecting a card, or tickets to a concert, or a gift certificate, or backstage passes, or . . .

"A bill?" You shouldn't have. "Oh, the tea stain. Sorry again about that. Thanks. For this." I wave the flimsy paper.

"Your mom insisted." And then Keiko gives me a wink—her big we-have-a-secret wink. I don't know why until she stands up. "I'll leave you two alone," she says in a low voice.

Us two?

From behind me, I hear Jeremy's voice: "Hi, Jessica. C'mon, check out these ice sculptures they've got in the back."

Lame excuse to get away from the crowd?

I'm on it.

Jeremy and I slip away from the group and around the corner to where the caterers are keeping the ice sculptures. The sculptures are in different shapes: a heart for love, clasped hands for faith, and an ice fountain that spells out LOLA BANKS along the base and is burbling water.

I can hear Hélène's voice in my head: "So much money, so little taste." (I was worried about flashing the fake tiara in the Bankses' faces, and that was Hélène's response. "That sort does not know shiny from Shinola." Which sounded especially odd in a French accent.)

After all the excitement, it's nice to have a quiet moment.

"Mission accomplished." I can't help smiling. "We righted the wrongs, caught Kenny the criminal, and all around saved the day. What's left for us to do?"

"I can think of one thing," says Jeremy, very quietly. He takes my hands in his, pulling me away from the frozen heart and toward his own. I look up at him and—

"Jessica! There you are. It's the real DVD. I checked!" Jeremy and I startle apart. "I wanted . . ." My sister pauses for a moment and looks at us. "Um, let's celebrate later," she says, awkwardly retreating.

I'm almost as surprised as Eva.

For the first time ever, I had forgotten she was in the room.

The rest of the night is a blast. A dessert buffet of honey-roasted Asian pears and chocolate-dipped orange wedges gets rolled out along with the ice sculptures. A small band takes the stage.

Mom and Dad are some of the first people on the dance floor. My dad is rocking his signature move: "driving the truck." He has both hands on an imaginary steering wheel, takes one hand off the wheel to change gear, goes back to steering, and then pulls on the imaginary air horn. Repeat while mixing in elements of "walking the dog," "making the pizza," and "doing the shopping." Rhythmic doesn't really describe it. Sometimes even I can't believe Dad's Latino! Mom is having a great time—not a great time in any way related to the music, but still a great time.

Where did I ever get my cool?

I spot a surprising face on the dance floor. Raúl Hernandez.

Jeremy explained to me that Raúl was a tutor-actor. He'd been hanging around hoping to get a part on the show—which he recently did. Angry Guy on Sidewalk. That's why he sounded so "upset" in Eva's dressing room when I overheard them. Well, the angry is gone and he's got some bounce in his boogie tonight!

I decide to join Mom and Dad. They need to see how dancing is done.

"This reminds me of the night we met," I hear Dad yell to Mom over the music.

"At the church picnic?" I ask.

He turns to drive the truck in my direction. "What? I met your mom at Disco Dan's Groove Hut. We just told Abuela it was at a church picnic." He sees the look on my face. "Um . . . and maybe we told you that, too."

Whoa . . . even parents have secrets. Horrible, horrible secrets. But the night has turned out too well to be tainted by my disco-related roots.

Paige joins us on the dance floor. Then Eva and Lavender. Then Lighting Guy Bob. Everyone starts driving the truck. *Beep! Beep!*

It takes a moment before I notice Paige is dancing with Jeremy. I'm keeping one eye on him, but the music changes as I'm mid-spin, and I don't know where he's gone. A slow song comes on.

Jeremy appears at my shoulder. He doesn't say anything. He takes me in his arms and begins to dance.

"Wow! You're a good dancer," I say.

He half-smiles. "I was in a traveling show of *The Nutcracker* for a while when I was a kid."

I'm reminded again that Jeremy's history of road shows, fast-food commercials, and movies-of-the-week comes with an assortment of unexpected skills.

"This is so much better than that lame fina*lei* party we had last season," he says.

"Finale party?"

"Finale-fina*lei*—it had a Hawaiian theme." I had a big test that night and couldn't go with E. I will not admit that solving the mystery of the cozy Jeremy-Lavender luau pictures makes me almost as happy as catching Kenny.

Jeremy pulls me up closer against his crisp shirt. It's nice to dance with him, shivery nice.

"May I cut in?" I know that voice. It comes with a barrel chest. Right now, it also comes with a frown.

"Of course, Mr. Ortiz."

Of all the times for Dad not to be under the hood of an old car! Jeremy gracefully backs away.

"So who is this Jones boy?" Dad asks gruffly. "Your mother says he's *around* a lot. What does that mean?"

"I don't know. What did it mean when you were my age?"

"Oh, no," Dad groans. He's quiet for a bit. Then he says, "You used to tell me everything."

"I used to tell Mom everything, and then she told you everything."

"Those were good times," Dad says.

I look around, seeing Eva and Mom laughing together; Jeremy dancing with his mom, watching me over her head. Even Keiko is on the floor, dancing with Roman and putting a smile on his face. And I didn't even know his lips could turn up.

My dad dances with me, old movie–style, around the room. "These are good times too," I tell him.

I sneak one last peek at Jeremy. He'd better rest up for tomorrow. His dream is about to come true.

*R*eclining on our white loungers, Mom, Eva, and I are enjoy-ing a well-earned rest by the pool.

Jeremy Jones is not.

"Tell me again why *Teen People*'s It Boy is mowing my lawn?" Mom asks.

"He's fulfilling a lifelong dream." I take a sip from my pink lemonade. "Plus he lost a bet."

Jeremy didn't think Kenny could be the culprit. In his mind, Kenny just didn't fit the part. (Maybe that's because I didn't tell Jeremy *all* the evidence . . . but still, there should be a doubting-Jessica penalty.)

"What did you have to do if you lost?"

"Buy us another lunch at the commissary."

"*Another* lunch?" Mom looks at Eva. "Your sister is getting en-tirely too mysterious lately."

"I know," E says. "I think it suits her."

I give her a smile.

"Are you sure you don't want to go to the Spilt Sugar concert with me tonight?" she asks. Paige and Kenny's tickets wound up in Eva's possession. Because that's the kind of life E leads.

"I'm sure. Take Keiko. She'll love it." And she deserves it.

Mom sighs. "I can't believe you're making Jeremy push that old mower."

"Well, Dad won't let us throw it out, and the gardeners never touch it. I thought it could use a workout."

And then, to prove that some things do happen in life the way you'd script them: A girl in a white tennis shirt and skirt appears along the path between our houses. (Confession: I did ask Jeremy to come over at the same time as the daily tennis lesson.)

Tennis Neighbor drops her racket. "Is that Jeremy Jones? Is he your . . . lawn boy?"

Maybe I was hoping she would walk by. Would notice him. Maybe I'd been planning my response.

"Well, we don't own him. We only *rent* his services."

She stares and stares and stumbles back to her house. She doesn't even pick up her racket.

I can't resist snapping a cell phone pic of Jeremy sweating over the mower. I send it to Leo along with this message:

Avenger, don't worry
about Poet. Helping to
bring some of the
Hollywood heads back
to their (grass) roots.
Call me. Have some
story ideas. Poet.

My brand-new school doesn't seem quite so scary at the moment. Having rescued Eva from an image assassin, I may be able to handle the challenges of fitting in at a Beverly Hills private school. Plus my luck is completely turning around. *Two Sisters'* most recent guest stars walked away from the set under their own power; Mary-Kate said that whole flying-elbows-on-the-dance-floor thing could have happened to anybody.

Twenty minutes later (I told you, Bev Hills lawns are small), Jeremy is sweaty and grass-stained, and if Gap made an ad of him right now, people would want to buy the whole sweaty, grass-stained look. That's Hollywood for you.

I pour Jeremy a glass of lemonade, and we dangle our feet in the pool. Petunia is at my side, panting at her reflection.

"How did your *TeenDream* interview go?" Ever since the haircut, Jeremy has been getting more press coverage than ever.

"The usual. I got to talk about Heifer.org's Donate-a-Duck charity for a minute, and then they wanted to know all about my love life."

"Did you tell them what kind of girl you like?"

"Yep."

"So, spill."

"She's got brown hair, brown eyes, likes dogs, and wears a sun hat with a red band."

"Pretty specific, aren't you?" I peek at him from under the brim of my red-banded sun hat.

"Unfortunately, she's also the kind of girl who needs things spelled out in billboard-sized letters."

"Not the brightest star in the sky, huh?"

"That's the way I like 'em."

"Jeremy, why'd you put up with all my madness?"

Jeremy smiles. "Everyone I meet is pretending to be somebody else—some of us get paid a lot of money to do it. But you, Jessica Ortiz, are just trying to be you."

I feel a one-word poem coming on:

Happy

Down through the hills, I can see the lights flickering on all over the studio lots and soundstages of L.A. But for tonight, it's nice to be just Jessica, starring in my own life, with very special guest star Jeremy Jones.

EXTERIOR SHOT: SLOPES OF BEVERLY HILLS. POOLSIDE AT SPANISH-STYLE HOUSE. TWO FIGURES MOVE TOGETHER AGAINST THE BRILLIANT RED AND ORANGE SKY.
FADE OUT.

Happily Eva After

Our spywitness Keiko shares scoop on TV teen Eva Ortiz's supersecret skill: crime catching! The brown-eyed beauty scripted the act that nabbed a *Two Sisters* set thief. Will Eva give up acting for detecting? Now that would be a crime!

$\mathcal{H}$ ere are three clues to where author Mary Wilcox lives: *Legally Blonde* was filmed there. *Sabrina, the Teenage Witch* was set there. Celebrities Uma Thurman, Matt Damon, and Paul Revere were born there.   ;)

Visit www.hollywoodsisters.com for more information.

PSST! DON'T MISS THE NEXT BOOK IN
THE *Hollywood Sisters* SERIES

Los Angeles! Mexico! Wisconsin?

*R*eal life isn't *reel* life, right? At least that's what Jeremy Jones tried to tell me after his red carpet smoochfest with Paige. Not. Buying. It.

Besides, I'm too busy drinking in all the local color (from Mayan ruins to Cheeseheads!) as part of my sister E's entourage . . . and digging deep to find out who's behind the mysterious mishaps on the *Two Sisters* set. Because all roads seem to be leading back to (big gulp) . . . yours truly.